Lethal
OBSESSION

DOBI CROSS

Luxhaven
Publishing

ISBN paperback, 978-1-958987-10-0

Interior & Cover Design by Luxhaven Publishing

Editing by JD Book Services

To JC, Grandma D, and DC, whom I love more than life itself.

AUTHOR'S NOTE

Thank you for choosing LETHAL OBSESSION.
Zora Smyth was a character I was fortunate to meet a
couple of months ago as I brainstormed ideas for my
first medical thriller story for an anthology.

LETHAL OBSESSION continues the story of Zora
Smyth as she's accused of murder and has to deal
with the implications of that in the US justice system.
We see how Zora is able to remain true to who she is
through this trying time in her life, and the impor-
tance she places on family and friends.

It was important for me as I penned this series to
have Zora Smyth not be some super hero or a person
with extraordinary abilities, but an everyday person

who through the journey of the next few books comes to fully understand and appreciate who she truly is and is able to heal from the childhood baggage she's carried all her life.

Please continue this journey with me in LETHAL RECONCILIATION. You can grab your copy at https://dobicross.com.

Would you also want to be notified when the next Dobi Cross book releases? Sign up at https://dobi-cross.com.

Once again, thank you so much for purchasing LETHAL OBSESSION and for meeting Zora Smyth. If you enjoyed it, please consider leaving a review at your favorite retailer or recommending it to a friend.

Thanks again for your support!

Dobi Cross

Lethal
OBSESSION

1

"I'm sorry. I'm so sorry," the young woman whimpered as she struggled to free herself from the chains that bound her to the operating table. But it was no use—she was Thomas Stewart's canvas, chosen to be his masterpiece like all the other girls before her.

Fear oozed from her pores as he watched her beg for his mercy. But the usual euphoria that ignited his skin and snaked through his veins was missing. Stewart's jaw clenched as he guessed why.

It was all because of Dr. Zora Smyth.

She'd caused her friend and detective, Dave McKesson, to poke his nose in Stewart's organ trafficking business, and the guy had refused to let go, like a dog that had found a good bone. So Stewart had stopped him by making Zora take the fall for the murder of Dr. Edwards, Stewart's business associate in the trafficking business, and Zora's former mentor. *That should keep the detective busy for a while*, he mused.

But Stewart had underestimated how much Zora had become a drug in his veins, causing an itch he couldn't scratch and dousing the customary high he'd always enjoyed from transforming each girl into his painting.

He grimaced and glanced down at the surgical instrument his gloved hand had reached for. It was the bone hammer he kept nearby for special requests. Stewart studied it for a minute, turning it over and over in his hand, and then he sent it spinning across the room where it crashed against the wall and landed on the floor.

Yet the action didn't assuage his anger at Zora Smyth.

She'd ruined everything.

The pungent smell of urine filled the air as it dripped from the table onto the floor, bringing Stewart back to the present. He'd forgotten about the girl for a moment, and now she'd made a mess of his canvas.

Stewart's nose twitched, and his eyes narrowed. It was a sin he couldn't forgive.

"Please, I'm sorry," the girl pleaded repeatedly, her cries burning into Stewart's mind and agitating the rage that simmered under the surface.

Stewart tensed. He'd teach this girl a lesson, just like Zora would learn after he was done with her. She'd bossed him around, believing she was after all his chief surgical resident at the hospital. Instead, he'd had her on a string all along, one she'd tried to cut by messing with him. So Stewart had punished her, just like he was about to do to the girl before him.

He picked up the scalpel and went to work, making a vertical midline incision from the xiphoid process to the symphysis pubis and tearing apart the peritoneum to reach her organs. A primal scream tore from the girl's throat, echoing in the chamber long after she'd gone silent from the shock. But Stewart kept at it, dissecting until he couldn't see straight from all the blood that clouded his vision.

His anger spent, Stewart dropped the scalpel into a surgical bowl and looked down at the mix of blood, peritoneal fluid, and pieces of organ tissue on his gloved hands and then at the girl's remains splayed on the table.

He'd only planned to retrieve the girl's kidneys and liver, but now he'd made a mess of everything, even as the pungent smell of blood and fecal matter filled the air.

Still, he felt no release.

His nostrils flared. All because of Zora. All because Stewart hadn't accounted for the possibility that she'd change his desires.

He'd spent so much time with Zora at the hospital that he'd grown a longing to own her, to have the feisty doctor in his grip, ready to do his bidding, that it now appeared that was what he needed to get some release.

Stewart banged a clenched fist on the table, and the surgical bowl upturned, its contents scattering across the table's surface and over the remains of the body in front of him. There was no way he could salvage the girl's organs now, and he'd need a new girl donor to meet his business demands on time, though he was sure Erik, his right-hand man and bodyguard, had already made plans for that.

But Stewart was due at the hospital shortly for his night float duty, and there was no way he could continue working in the room's current condition without a clean-up. The room stank, causing a sour taste to fill Stewart's mouth.

Stewart pressed a button on the wall, a signal to

Erik to come in and restore the chamber to its pristine condition.

The organs would have to wait.

But the plan to own Zora Smyth was already in motion.

Stewart smiled at the thought. It was time for the cat-and-mouse game with Zora to begin.

2

D

r. Zora Smyth shook her head, hoping what was happening to her right now was only a dream. If it was, she was having a hard time waking up. She couldn't believe that only a few weeks ago, she'd been looking in from the other side of this interrogation room.

Zora let out a sigh as she cinched her coat tighter around herself. She hadn't had time to change from her white tank top and gray capri pants when the police officers had arrested her at home for the murder of her long-time mentor, Dr. Edwards, so she'd donned a coat instead. They'd even denied her request to call her lawyer, AKA Mom.

The drive in the squad car back to the station had taken longer than usual, with the driver meandering through busy streets instead of taking the easy, straight route. By the time they'd arrived, what should have been a twenty-minute drive had taken two hours—the clock on the wall had said four-thirty p.m. as the detectives led Zora into the interview room.

She'd been in a daze while they'd fingerprinted her, snapped her picture, and taken away her personal belongings. Now she sat opposite Dave's partner and another man, a short, potbellied man with thinning hair and sad eyes overshadowed by crow's feet, who Zora didn't recognize. The heady mix of cigarette smoke, day-old coffee, and air freshener that permeated the air wasn't helping.

Zora fought hard to maintain a steady façade as she took a deep breath and exhaled to calm herself. They were probably recording everything, and she had no plans to give them anything they could use against her. She'd done nothing wrong and didn't deserve to be here. *God, help me*.

The door swung open as Detective Dave, her almost boyfriend, barged in.

Zora's eyes lit up, and her body relaxed. She'd never been so glad to see him. Maybe he could make them realize this was all a mistake—there was no way she'd murdered Dr. Edwards. Zora hadn't seen

Dr. Edwards since his arrest for kidnapping her. She'd spent a few days in the hospital and then the week after recuperating at home. Besides, she had no motive to kill him as far as she could tell.

Dave's face was a mask of fury, the pain of betrayal clear in his eyes. "What's going on here?" he asked as his eyes darted from his partner to the other cop.

"Detective McKesson, I need you to leave," the second cop said without preamble.

"Lieutenant—"

"Now," the man insisted in a commanding tone.

Zora's face crumpled. It seemed this second cop outranked Dave, and that didn't bode well for her.

"And for goodness' sake, lose that ridiculous tie," the man finished.

Zora's eyes swung to the aforementioned tie, and her breath caught in her throat. She recognized it— the rainbow paw-prints tie had been a gift from her mom to Dave on the day of their high school dance, which had also been a fund-raising event for the local animal shelter. Zora had laughed at the tie that day and said it would always remind her of her mom. So why was he wearing it now? *Think, Zora, think.*

Her eyes widened. Dave was trying to tell her he'd reached out to her mom!

Zora's shoulders relaxed, and she gave Dave a tiny smile.

He exhaled, relief mirrored in his eyes that she'd gotten the message. Then Dave turned to his partner and gave him a disgusted look before leaving the room and shutting the door behind him.

The lieutenant turned back to Zora. "Dr. Zora Smyth, I'm Lieutenant Bandy. We've arrested you for the murder of Dr. Edwards, the man you probably hate, since he deceived and kidnapped you. I'm sure you're aware you have the right to remain silent and anything you say can be used against you in a court of law. You have the right to consult an attorney before speaking to the police, and to have an attorney present during questioning now or in the future. If you cannot afford an attorney, one will be appointed for you before any questioning if you wish, and if you decide to answer questions now without an attorney present, you still have the right to stop answering at any time until you speak with an attorney."

Zora straightened in her chair and squared her shoulders. "I want my lawyer."

"Dr. Smyth, why did you kill Dr. Edwards?"

Zora still had a hard time believing he was dead, but she knew better than to ask or answer questions the cops had. "I want my lawyer," she insisted.

The lieutenant banged a stack of papers on the bolted table between them, causing Zora to jump, but she recovered and affected a bored look.

"I'm not sure you understand the gravity of the situation here," the man said. "Where were you this morning between ten a.m. and eleven a.m.?"

Zora said nothing and stared at the cream-colored wall that seemed to have received a fresh coat of paint since the last time she'd been here. She could see a muscle twitch in Dave's partner's jaw as the burly detective typed into a laptop in front of him.

The lieutenant repeated the question, but Zora had already zoned out and instead focused on her mom's impending arrival.

As if on command, the door swung open, and a tall, thin man in a black leather jacket stepped into the interview room and whispered something into the lieutenant's ear. The lieutenant looked up at him and then at Zora. Then he turned to Dave's partner. "Have you finished with the statement?" he asked.

"Yes, I've sent it to you," Dave's partner replied.

"Good. Take her to lockup." The lieutenant got up and walked out of the room.

Dave's partner led Zora to a holding cell with

three other occupants—two women in their thirties who looked like they'd been around this block a few times and a young woman in her early twenties crouched in a corner with her head down in her lap. She didn't react when Dave's partner pushed Zora in and slammed the metal bar door behind her.

Zora avoided eye contact with all three ladies and headed to an unoccupied section of the tiny cell. The place stunk, and Zora forced back the bile that rose in her throat. She tucked herself into a corner and let her head fall back against the dirty wall.

This was so unreal. Murder? How could they even think she was the culprit? She had no reason to kill Dr. Edwards, despite what the cops had said. It had to be a mistake. But a judge wouldn't have issued an arrest warrant unless they had some sort of evidence, and there was no way they could have any unless…

She sat up. Was that what was happening here? Planted evidence?

"Hey, you!" a voice called out.

Zora didn't respond.

"I'm talking to you, rich kid."

Zora looked across the cell in the voice's direction to see the two women glaring at her. She? A kid? Zora was likely only a few years younger than them.

"Yes, I'm talking to you," said the one with unwashed stringy blonde hair tied off by a dirty ribbon, while the other glowered at her.

Zora said nothing and looked away. She had no beef with them or any reason to make matters worse for herself in this place. 'Keep your head down and mind your business' in a place like this was the one thing she'd learned from Marcus—her beloved friend and big brother—and from his juvie stories.

"Oh, no she didn't!" The blonde-haired woman jumped to her feet, her face distorted by a sneer.

The hair on Zora's arms rose. This was a confrontation she didn't want, yet Zora stayed alert all the same. For all she knew, the woman had a weapon on her that the cops hadn't picked up on.

Then the woman lurched toward Zora.

3

D ave closed the door of the interview room behind him. He still couldn't believe they'd arrested Zora for the murder of Dr. Edwards. Hadn't it only been yesterday when he'd rescued her from the hands of Dr. Edwards and the cartel after she'd dug into their activities to save her friend and roommate Christina?

Now, it seemed the tables had turned on her, with his partner, Trevor, serving as the catalyst and betraying Dave.

It hurt to think about it. Trevor and Dave had been partners for over four years. In that time, they'd faced many life-and-death situations together and had bonded like brothers. Dave had become part of Trevor's family and was even a godfather to one of his kids. Trevor had known Dave and Zora were close—though he did not know how much—so going behind his back and arresting her had been like a stab in the heart. Trevor should have given Dave a heads up, even if he couldn't ignore the order from the lieutenant.

Good thing another officer who knew Dave had been involved in Zora's kidnapping case had called him as soon as he heard about the arrest. Dave had the day off and had been on his way to her apartment for lunch when he'd gotten the call. He'd been too far away to intervene, so he'd called Zora's mom, but had gotten her voicemail instead. He'd only reached her a few minutes ago. She'd been in court for an out-of-town case and had left as soon as she'd gotten his message. She'd also sent a lawyer from her firm to the station to handle the case until she got in.

But Dave couldn't wait until they arrived. He had to help Zora, and he would start by finding out all he could about the case.

He hastened to his desk in the homicide unit, a medium-sized room on the east side of the station. Dave's large desk occupied a prime corner of the room and was void of the usual knickknacks common to most officers who'd had their desks for many years. Instead, it had twin mountains of paperwork stacked on each end like sentries on duty.

Dave sat down and logged into his computer to access the records management system that housed all the station's information, records, or files pertaining to its law enforcement operations. Within a few seconds, he found Zora's case file and clicked on it.

A restricted access notice flashed on his computer screen.

That's strange. He tried again and got the same result.

Dave banged his fist on the desk, and sheets of paper fluttered from the stacks onto the floor. A few officers in the unit looked up from what they were doing, and he gave them an apologetic smile. Soon they returned their eyes back to their work.

He picked up the stray sheets from the floor, returned them to their stacks, and leaned back in his chair. What was going on here? He'd always had access to every homicide case in their station, given his ranking. So why was this case different?

Calm down, Dave, and think. Was there something about this case they didn't want him to know? Fine, he had a personal relationship with Zora. But he'd always kept his personal life separate from his professional one, a principle his colleagues knew he stood by. If Zora had broken the law, Dave would make sure she turned herself in, even though he'd stand by her side all the way. So, if they'd locked him out of the files, it was possible something was wrong with the case.

Dave rubbed his jaw. In fact, he'd been getting strange vibes since he's heard about her arrest, from the way they'd arrested Zora, to the way the officers involved were keeping everything hush hush, and now this. The case had a rotten smell to it, similar to what he'd experienced in another case in New York, where someone had been pulling the strings from behind the scenes.

Was that the same situation here? But why would anyone want to frame her for the murder of Dr. Edwards?

Dave's mind raced. The only motive he could think of was the missing kidneys case, but Zora had disengaged herself from it once they'd rescued her and Christina. He was the only one working on it now.

He straightened as a thought struck him, his breath catching in his throat, and a coldness hitting his core. Could it be because of him? He'd tried to run his investigation under the radar, keeping it from his lieutenant—Dave had heard rumors he had connections to the city's deep pockets, so he'd refrained from updating him about it. Only one person had been privy to the information. Trevor.

A muscle in Dave's jaw twitched. He would have thought it impossible for his partner to be involved, but now he wasn't so sure. Trevor had always been clean as a whistle, but his daughter had been going through some health challenges, and Dave knew the bills had piled up. Yet it wasn't enough reason to throw someone else's child under the bus and ruin the rest of her life.

Dave stood. He couldn't sit here waiting. Trevor had some explaining to do, and Dave needed to talk to him right now.

He hurried to the interview room. Hopefully, the lieutenant should have left by now, leaving Trevor in charge, and Dave would catch him there.

The door was ajar, and Dave pushed it wide open. But the room was empty.

Dave's thoughts whirled. Why? The interview process was typically lengthy, and Trevor should still have been here. Had something hurried them along?

His first instinct was to check up on Zora—they'd probably taken her to a holding cell—but pursuing Trevor seemed like the better option. Dave needed an insight into the case to help her, which was what she needed most, and chances were Trevor had been the one to take Zora to lockup. This way, he could kill two birds with one stone.

Another officer in uniform passed by with a cup of coffee, and Dave stopped him.

"Have you seen Trevor?" he asked.

The officer, a young man with pale blue eyes, gestured toward the exit. "I just saw him leaving."

"Thank you." Good thing Dave had asked. He had to catch up to Trevor before he disappeared.

Dave sprinted toward the exit. He swiped his access card at the door and hastened outside. The cool air brushed his skin, but it was nothing he couldn't handle without a coat. He scanned the parking lot and saw someone who looked like Trevor, with his sandy blonde hair, driving Dave's and Trevor's squad car out of the parking lot.

Dave sprinted to his personal car, reversed it, and raced after Trevor. By the time Dave got on the two-lane road, Trevor's car was already two intersections ahead of him. Dave drove as quickly as he could within speed limits and narrowed the gap to about four cars between them.

Calling Trevor on the phone to ask him to stop was out of the question—Trevor could use that excuse to disappear. It was best to catch him off guard, though Trevor might have guessed by now that Dave would come after him about the case. Just when Dave thought he'd caught up to him, a big trailer joined the traffic a car ahead of him and slowed to a stop as the traffic light changed from green to red.

Dave fidgeted. He craned his neck and saw Trevor's car make a right turn at the next major intersection. There was a popular cafe off that road where cops liked to grab food. He hoped Trevor was headed there.

He finger-tapped the steering wheel as he waited for the light to change. *Come on, come on.* He couldn't afford to lose him now. The traffic light changed to green, and soon he reached the intersection. He turned onto the road and was at the cafe within a minute. He could see the squad car parked in a corner and someone talking on the phone in it.

Thank goodness. Dave parked, got out, and strode to the squad car. He tapped his fingers on the passenger window, showing his face and keep his hands visible. The tinted window wound down, and Dave saw an unexpected face staring back at him.

"Freddy, what are you doing in the squad car?" Fred had joined their unit a few weeks ago and had no partner yet.

Fred's face flushed, and he cleared his throat. "The lieutenant assigned me as Trevor's new partner."

Dave stiffened. What did that mean? "Since when?"

"Since this morning, sir. I assumed you knew about it."

There had been no mention of it, not from the lieutenant and not from Trevor. And where did that put Dave? One more thing to take up with the lieutenant later. But that could wait—finding Trevor was more important. "Where's Trevor?" he asked Fred.

"Back at the station. He's supposed to go with the transport wagon."

Dave's heart quickened. The transport wagon typically went out later in the day. If it was leaving now, then they'd take Zora too.

He had to get back to the station now.

Dave raced back to his car.

4

"Sit down, Susan!" a passing cop barked out to the woman in the cell. "Unless you have plans to stay with us longer this time."

The woman held up her hands and backed away from Zora. "I was doing nothing," she said.

"Let's make sure it stays that way." The cop eyed Zora and then turned away.

The woman gave Zora a nasty look, but said nothing else.

Zora let out a sigh of relief. She hadn't even realized she'd been holding her breath. Now she'd have to watch her back until this nightmare was over.

The cell felt chilly, and Zora wrapped her arms around herself. She'd never felt so alone. It was like she'd been cut off from the rest of the world. And where was Dave? She'd expected him to check on her by now.

Her heart raced. This was no time for a panic attack. She needed her wits about her. *I can get through this. I can get through this,* she thought to herself. She took a deep inhale and exhaled, but it wasn't working. She repeated the routine a couple more times before she felt the panic receding and her heart beginning to calm.

"Get up!" a voice barked.

Zora looked up to see a rotund officer in a police uniform, with another by his side, gesturing at them. Zora didn't know what was going on, but it seemed the others did. Soon, they'd handcuffed Zora and the other women and escorted them out of the building. Zora kept looking back. Where was Dave?

She turned to the officer closest to her. "Where are we going?" she asked him, but the man ignored her and prodded her to move along. Zora tripped and then righted herself. She hadn't realized until now how important free hands were in maintaining balance.

"We're going to county jail," a soft voice said from behind her. Zora turned her head. She hadn't noticed her.

It was the quiet young woman.

5

Dave's tires screeched as he entered the police station's parking lot. A vehicle had broken down on his side of the road, causing traffic to slow to a crawl and delaying his return. Dave hoped he hadn't missed the prisoner transport.

He jumped out of his car and looked around for the paddy wagon. It wasn't in its usual spot, which meant it was already in use. But where was it? Then he saw a colleague of his who helped with prisoner transport heading to the station's rear entrance.

Dave sprinted and caught up with him. "Simon, has the paddy left?"

The grizzly guy with the broken nose and black

hawk eyes turned to Dave and nodded. "A few minutes ago."

"Did they take everyone?"

"Yes, including the young doctor. Trevor went with them." Simon turned away and continued walking.

Dave's heart dropped. He'd just missed both Zora and Trevor.

He ran his hands through his hair. This was crazy. Today was not going as planned.

Dave pulled out his phone to call Trevor, but the number rang through with no one answering. Dave tried a couple more times, and on his third redial, the call went straight to voicemail.

His nostrils flared, and he ran a hand through his hair again. He kicked a soda can that was on the pavement, and it clattered off and then rolled to a stop a few feet away. So Trevor was avoiding him. But he couldn't hide forever; Dave would eventually catch up with him.

But sweet Zora. He'd let her down. Everything that was happening to her was because of him. She had to be in shock and scared, though he'd bet she wouldn't show it. She must be wondering why he hadn't come to see her, and now he wouldn't get that chance for the next forty-eight hours. If only he'd been on the case.

His phone rang. He pulled it from his pocket and checked the screen. It was Zora's mom.

Dave swiped the green button. "Hello, Mrs. Smyth."

"How's Zora?"

"They've taken her to the county jail."

There was a quick inhale from the other end of the line. "What about the lawyer? Has he arrived? I gave him your number to call as soon as he did."

"I've seen no one. Maybe he's stuck in traffic." At that moment, a silver Mercedes Benz arrived in the parking lot and parked a few feet from the entrance. A young man in a crisp suit stepped out, holding a black briefcase. "Does the lawyer have ginger hair?"

"Yes, he does."

"He just arrived."

"Okay, I'll call him now. I just landed at the airport and will head straight to the county jail. I should be there in about forty-five minutes. Let me know if you find out anything."

"Sounds good." The line went dead.

Dave looked to see the young lawyer answering a call. Zora's mom would take it from here.

He, on the other hand, planned to make the best use of the next forty-eight hours to find out all he could about the case.

6

The solid metal door of the cell clanged shut with finality behind Zora. She was in jail, her freedom cut off. Zora had never imagined she'd find herself here.

They'd processed her and given her two sheets, a pillow, and a thin blanket at intake. Zora now placed those items on the thin mattress lying on the steel bed's lower bunk. They'd also assigned the quiet young woman she'd met at lockup to the same cell as her and she'd already claimed the upper bed. She hadn't said another word to Zora since she'd spoken on the way to jail.

Zora looked around at her new home. It was about a third of her bedroom size and was sparse, with an all-in-one sink-toilet made of stainless steel.

They painted the walls a dull cream color, though some sections were now stained with dark streaks—Zora chose not to imagine what those could be.

A faint nasty smell emanated from the toilet, and Zora's stomach churned at the thought of using it. It probably had hundreds of germs on its surface, which could only get worse with use. Then there was the lack of privacy. But there was nothing she could do about both.

Zora made her bed and climbed in with her back against the wall. Her lower lip quivered, and she choked back a cry. This was her worst nightmare coming to life. Zora couldn't imagine having to spend the rest of her life in a place like this.

She drew in a tremulous breath. She could survive this. *God, help me.*

Her eyes swept to her left, and she noticed some markings on the wall beside her head. Zora studied the scribblings and gasped.

Someone, presumably a former occupant of this cell, had scratched out a hex, cursing to death whoever stayed in that cell!

Zora's hands clenched into fists, and holy anger rose within her. Whoever wrote this had no right! No curse had any power over her, and she wouldn't die no matter what she ended up facing in this jail. She'd get out of here. But first Zora needed to figure out who was behind everything.

She didn't need a prophecy to know that someone had framed her for the murder. The person, most likely Dr. Edwards' killer, had to be someone powerful enough to have moved the prosecutor to request an arrest warrant and get Dave's partner to betray him—Dave's expression in the interrogation room had confirmed it.

Someone that influential could also have long tentacles that reached into this jail, which meant Zora had to always be on guard. She couldn't trust anyone, no matter how nice they appeared. It was exhausting just to think of it, but it might be the only way Zora could survive this hellhole.

"Smyth, you have a visitor," a correctional officer yelled.

Zora turned away from the hex, scrambled down from her bed, and stood, tucking her long dark wavy hair behind her ears. The cell door opened, and the CO came in and snapped handcuffs on her. Another CO stood by the door, watching. They led Zora down the long hallway to a light gray door. One of the COs opened the door for her and motioned for her to sit in the single bolted-down chair visible from the doorway. Zora stepped into the room and looked across the glass at her visitor.

Her mom, Adrianna Smyth, had arrived!

She looked beautiful, as always, with her delicate mixed-heritage features and honey-colored blonde hair. People always thought she'd been a beauty queen, but behind it all lay a keen intelligent mind, one that had built Smyth Law Associates from nothing to what it was today. But worry lines Zora had never seen creased her mom's forehead today.

Zora let out a sigh, like she'd rolled off a heavy burden, and her shoulders relaxed. She'd be alright as long as her mom was here. She moved over to the chair and sat down, her eyes never leaving her mom's. The CO removed her handcuffs and then stepped out of the room, shutting the door behind her. Her mom motioned to her to pick up the phone that hung on the glass partition that separated them. Zora lifted the phone and held it against her ear. Her mom did the same.

"I'm sorry," her mom said, concern written all over her face. "For being late."

Zora's eyes brimmed with tears. It felt so good to be with someone familiar, someone who understood her without her having to say the words.

"I didn't get Dave's message on time," her mom

continued. "I was in the courtroom for an out-of-town case, and the judge had insisted all phones be switched off. If I had, I would have gotten one of my lawyers to handle it until I arrived. I'm sorry."

"It's okay," Zora said.

"How are you doing?" her mom asked softly.

"I'm hanging in there," Zora responded. "It still feels unreal."

"I'm going to get you out of here, okay?"

Zora nodded. She and her mom hadn't always been close, and they were still working on their relationship. But she trusted her mom. She always meant whatever she said.

"Can you tell me what happened?" her mom asked. Zora's eyes searched the ceiling. "There are no recordings," her mom said. "I'm your lawyer on record, so the visits are confidential."

So Zora told her mom all that had happened from the time she'd opened her door to see the officers—the long trip to the station, the interview room and lockup, and her arrival at the county jail. "I thought it was weird how it took so long to get to the station when we could have taken a shorter route."

"Like they needed the delay."

"Yes. We ended up getting there around four-thirty p.m. A solid two-hour difference, which was ridiculous."

"And you asked for a lawyer, and they didn't give you the chance to call one?" her mom asked.

"Yes. It was like they ignored me even after they read me my Miranda rights."

Her mom's brow wrinkled. "Hmm. I think they were trying to make sure you couldn't post bail. That's the only reason that comes to mind, which means it's important for whoever was behind this to have you in jail over the weekend." Then she leaned forward. "Zora, listen to me. I need you to be super careful and on your guard. Don't make eye contact with anyone and stay on your own as much as possible."

Zora nodded. "Okay," she said.

"Look at me, Zora." Zora met her mom's gaze. She could see the encouragement and confidence in them. "It's okay to be scared. But you can survive this, even if you think otherwise. You have what it takes, trust me. I'll do everything I can to get you out of here first thing Monday morning."

Zora nodded again. She didn't trust herself to speak.

Her mom straightened. "I think my time is almost up. Unfortunately, I won't be able to check in with you tomorrow. They've denied our request for one of us to see you. But we'll be here on Sunday, okay?"

Zora gave her a small smile. She was glad she had her mom in her corner. Then she remembered. "Oh, you don't need to add any money to my name. I'm good."

"Are you sure?" her mom asked.

"I don't plan to stay long in this place."

"Okay, no money. Got it." Her mom gave her an encouraging smile. "Take care of yourself, Zora," she said.

The door buzzed, and the CO stepped back into the room. "Visiting time is over," he said.

Zora dropped the phone back in its cradle and got up from the chair. She gave her mom one last smile and then stepped out through the door.

This was the pep talk she'd needed. *I'm going to hang in there no matter what.* It was her life at stake, and no one had a right over it.

Zora would not let the perpetrator win.

7

Marcus Tate stood by his hotel window close to the Nelson Mandela square and looked down at the busy streets of central Johannesburg. A city built on gold mines, its skyscrapers dotted the city's skyline and created a tunnel-like effect amidst its narrow streets filled with colorful street art, a variety of small shops, and energetic street traders.

Men and women of all races and ethnicity hurried along the streets in this proud and friendly city. It was springtime here at this time of the year, and the sun glowed in the sky with no pregnant clouds in sight.

Marcus had arrived in the city a few weeks ago on behalf of Smyth Law Associates—Zora's mom's law firm—and had worked non-stop to close a business deal ahead of schedule. He planned to visit a potential client tomorrow and then explore the city for a few hours before his flight back home.

But he couldn't wait to get back to Lexinbridge.

He'd been upset at Zora's kidnapping and had cut short his visit to return early and make sure she was okay. Then he'd received news that they'd rescued her, and he'd stayed back to complete the rest of the business deal. But he was impatient to see her and confirm for himself that everything was alright.

Marcus had been by her side a few years ago when she'd discovered a murdered victim on her dissecting table and had helped her crack the case. They'd dated a few times after that, but Zora had opted to keep the relationship platonic. So Marcus had respected her wishes, and they'd gone their separate ways, though they'd stayed in touch over the years. But he still cared for her way much more than she could imagine.

His phone rang. Marcus turned away from the window and strode to the bedside table. He picked up the phone and sat on the bed to answer it. "Hello, boss." Zora's mom was his employer, but she also treated him like a son.

"Marcus, Zora needs you," Zora's mom said without preamble.

Marcus' heart rate quickened, and he sat up straight. Something terrible must have happened to Zora. "What's wrong?"

"They've arrested her for murder!" Zora's mom choked back a cry.

Marcus sprang to his feet. Impossible! Zora couldn't even harm a fly, had the greatest respect for human life, and did all she could to save her patients. How could the cops think someone like that had murdered anyone? The only explanation was that someone had it out for her and was determined to make her the culprit.

Zora's mom was silent for a moment, as if to pull herself together, before she continued. "She's in county jail, and they got her in for the weekend. So I can't bail her out until Monday."

"I'm on my way," Marcus said. "Everything is going to be alright."

"Thanks, Marcus. Let me know when you get in, okay?"

"I will." The line went dead.

Marcus checked to see if there were any available flights out of Johannesburg. He got a seat on one headed to New York later tonight, but it would still take about twenty-four hours before he'd reach Lexinbridge. A lot could happen to Zora in the county jail within those hours, especially given the circumstances of her recent case.

That was a risk he wasn't willing to take.

So Marcus picked his phone and dialed the one number he never thought he'd call.

8

Everyone always assumed Marcus had no living family, but he knew better—his past was a history he never liked to revisit. Marcus' father's family had always been poor, so his father and uncle had grown up the same way. So when they'd reached their early twenties, they'd both left home but went in separate directions.

Marcus' father had gotten a job in the city as a bus driver and on one of his routes had met his mother, who was a secretary for the city's department of law. They'd fallen in love, and Marcus had been born. His uncle Jimmy had chosen a life of crime and established his own crime family that, over the years, rivaled some of the biggest cartels in the area.

His father had disapproved of his uncle's life-style, so their family had distanced themselves from him. Marcus might not have dressed as well as some of his peers, but his home had been filled with lots of love. His parents had done their best to provide for him and always cheered him on. He'd been a constant fixture around his mother's workplace, and that was how the desire to work with the law had grown in him.

But all his dreams came crashing down when gunmen invaded their home and massacred his parents in cold blood. Marcus had been out shooting basketball with his friends when it happened and came home to see police cars parked all over his neighborhood. Something inside him had died that day when he'd learned his parents were dead. Later, rumors had circulated in his neighborhood that they murdered his parents for revenge, though no one knew why. Then his uncle had called him, sounding all broken and remorseful.

Marcus had realized the truth: his parents had died because of Uncle Jimmy.

After his parents' death, his Uncle Jimmy had wanted to take him in, but Marcus refused, preferring to run around with his own group. Zora's mom had met him in juvie, and the rest was history. He'd ended up working for her, eventually returning to school and graduating from college with a major in criminology and criminal justice. Marcus had gone back to work for her full-time and ended up as one of her lead investigators.

But he'd kept his distance from Uncle Jimmy over the years. No one, not even Zora's mom, knew about their relationship, since Marcus had wanted nothing to do with him.

Until now.

Zora needed protection in jail, and Uncle Jimmy was the one person who could provide it. Marcus was pretty sure his uncle had powerful connections in the justice system—he'd never been arrested and had even photographed with the best of them.

The phone rang and then connected. Uncle Jimmy had given him this number after his parents died—he said it was a special one only for Marcus. Marcus had never used it, though he'd saved the number.

He rose to his feet to take the call. "Uncle Jimmy, this is Marcus."

"I know. How can I help?"

Marcus' eyes widened. How had he guessed Marcus needed a favor?

His uncle chuckled as if he'd heard his unspoken question. "I know you wouldn't reach out unless it was a life-and-death situation."

"I have a friend who needs your protection," Marcus said.

"Zora Smyth?"

Marcus stiffened. "How did you know?"

"Let's just say I like to make sure my only blood family and nephew is safe. Consider it done. Is there anything else I can do for you about the case?"

"No, nothing. Just the protection."

"Okay, it's taken care of."

"Thank you."

"It's good to hear from you."

Marcus pulled at the collar of his shirt. "I have to go."

"Don't be a stranger, Marcus."

Marcus said nothing. This was all he'd wanted, and Uncle Jimmy owed him. There wouldn't be any need for them to connect after this. He ended the call.

He let out a sigh and sat on the bed, the room's air conditioning feeling cooler than before. Marcus hoped he wouldn't regret his decision to ask for his uncle's help, but there was no point worrying about that now. The deed was already done. Now, there would be other eyes on Zora, and his mind could be at ease.

But it was time to pack.

He had a plane ride to catch.

Zora woke up, feeling like she was underwater and desperate for air. She tried to breathe in and realized she couldn't, no matter how much she tried, with a semi-firm surface pressed over her nose and mouth.

She realized she was being suffocated with a pillow.

Zora fought against the pressure over her face, kicking out her limbs frantically to get much-needed air into her lungs, but the force pressing down on her chest was much stronger and frustrated her efforts. It was so torturous that escaping the pain and leaving her body behind seemed tempting.

Rivulets of sweat poured down her face as she continued to fight the panic. Her hands searched to grab the person holding her down, but only met air. Zora's brain was starving for oxygen. The surrounding sounds were fading, and nothing she did seemed to stop it. Her peripheral vision narrowed, and at that moment Zora knew she would lose consciousness first and then her life if she didn't stop what was happening. *God, please help me.*

Her hopes and dreams, family, and friends flashed before her eyes. She still had so much to live for, so much to accomplish. And no one had the right to take it away from her.

A sudden rage against the people trying to ruin and kill her filled her, and she pushed against the person with all the force she could muster. The individual crashed into the stainless-steel toilet, and a cry rang out.

Zora sat up, breathing hard, her lungs trying to gulp in as much oxygen as it could. She felt dizzy, but she shook her head to clear it away. Then she noticed her cellmate slumped beside the toilet and crying.

Her eyes widened. So she'd been the one trying to kill her! Why?

The cell door crashed open, and three COs stormed in. "What's going on?" the tallest one asked.

Zora pointed at her cellmate as she continued to

struggle to breathe. Her head pounded and her ears rang. "She… tried to… kill me."

Two COs grabbed the young lady by her arms. "I'm sorry, I'm sorry," she cried out as they pulled her up. "They have my baby." As if resigned to her fate, she let herself go limp as they hustled her out of the cell.

"Don't I get to see a doctor?" Zora asked the third CO in a hoarse voice as he turned to leave. "I need some oxygen."

The man leveled beady eyes on her. "I'm sure you'll be fine, *doctor*," he said and then locked the cell behind him.

Zora slumped against the wall and continued to take deep inhales and exhales. This was insane. She needed additional pure oxygen to minimize any chance of brain damage. And yet here they were, depriving her of her right to the care she deserved. The thick musty air was all she drew in, but she had no other choice. It would have to be enough.

Zora tucked herself into a corner of her bed, in a position that might help her stay awake. There was no way she could sleep tonight after what had just happened. What if they sent the young lady back to this cell? Another attempt from her might kill Zora.

But what had she meant by "they have my baby?"

Did someone send her to kill Zora? That was the only reason that made sense, since she hadn't met the girl before now. The cartel, who she suspected was behind this case, could do this. They probably had many eyes and ears in the jail and would hear about the girl's failure, which meant this might not be the last attack on Zora.

Zora fought the panic that threatened to rise within her. They didn't own her life or have the final say on whether she lived or died. God had saved her tonight, and He could do so again. Even if she had no friends or family here, she wasn't alone. She had to believe that.

So Zora wrapped her scratchy blanket around herself and prayed Monday would come soon.

10

"What do you mean someone tried to kill her?" Stewart's head jerked up from the body he'd been working on in his special chamber, the place where he carried out his experiments. The smell of roasted flesh filled the air from the cautery he'd used, but Stewart didn't pay it any attention—he was used to it.

"Her cellmate tried to smother her last night," Erik said.

Stewart's vision narrowed, and he dropped the forceps he'd been holding into a stainless-steel bowl. He'd only sent Zora to jail to break her and rattle her enough to stay out of his organ business, but he'd had no plans to kill her. "Who was it? Who sent the girl?"

"It was an order from Big Boss," Erik said.

Stewart stilled. Stewart's father, Anatoly Petrykin, was the *Pakhan* or head of the East European criminal enterprise in Lexinbridge. He ruled with an iron hand, and his word was law. "Why didn't I hear about it?"

"Vaslav passed down the order. I only overheard it when his boys were talking about it. Vaslav told Big Boss she'd been interfering with our business, so Big Boss asked him to get rid of her."

Stewart's jaw twitched. Vaslav—the stench in his nostrils he couldn't seem to get rid of. Vaslav was an *Avtoritet*, a brigadier in charge of the largest group in the family and Stewart's father's right-hand man. He did whatever it took to remain in that position and even fancied himself as the one to take over from Stewart's father someday, his current power only hampered by the two spies Big Boss kept by his side. Vaslav saw Stewart as a threat to his goals and held a deep disdain for him, which was reciprocated. He must have found out Stewart had his hand in the case and wanted to mess it all up.

Stewart picked back up the forceps and used it to tease apart the renal fascia that covered the kidney he was extracting. He would deal with Vaslav, but not now—he still needed him to handle some of the family's mundane tasks Stewart had no interest in. But Stewart would teach him a lesson in the meantime.

But first, he had to see his father and make sure he withdrew his order. Zora was his business and his alone. Nobody, not even his old man, had any right to interfere. Her cellmate shouldn't have accepted the job to touch what belonged to him.

He turned to Erik. "Get rid of the girl."

"Yes, boss."

11

Zora dragged her feet down the metal stairs that led to the jail's common area, that was surrounded by identical cells. She would have preferred to remain in her own cell, but the COs had denied her that option. She was bone-tired—she'd barely slept the rest of the night and had only pecked at her food this Saturday morning.

The common area was wide and filled with multiple bolted-down stainless-steel tables and chairs occupied by inmates. Zora tried not to gag at the potent smell of congealed body odors that hung low in the air. A single flatscreen TV secured by metal bars rested high on the wall, but only a few inmates were watching the comedy show that was airing. The rest were sitting around, doing nothing.

Zora had to be on her guard here. A simple look could get her killed. She scanned the area and found an empty spot away from everyone else, which suited her just fine. Zora made her way there, careful not to bump into anyone, and sat down. A few dust bunnies were on her table's surface, and she brushed them away before resting her elbows on it. She kept her eyes low—there was no need to court trouble. All she wanted was for time to come and go.

A diminutive chatterbox in her thirties with mousy brown hair who'd introduced herself as Sandy took the seat closest to hers. Zora ignored her and said nothing. She trusted no one and had no plans to start now, and it was best to mind her business. But the lady didn't seem to care and just kept yakking on and on.

Then the hair on Zora's skin rose, and her heart rate quickened. What danger could it be this time? She looked up to see a middle-aged woman with a short dark bob and matching dark eyes staring at her a few feet away on the right.

Zora averted her eyes. She couldn't recall meeting the woman before, and she didn't want trouble.

"That's Kelly," Sandy whispered from beside her. She must have noticed Zora's reaction. "She's here for murder. Killed her husband. But I heard her lawyers got it down to manslaughter. State was full, so they sent her here instead."

Zora shivered. Why her? She'd done nothing to catch the woman's interest. Or had the cartel sent her to finish the job? It was best to avoid her at all costs. Zora lowered her head, though she stayed alert.

But then her skin prickled worse than before. The scrutiny seemed to come from the far left side of the common space. She let out a sigh. Who was it this time? She'd hoped for a quiet mid-morning, but it seemed it was not to be. She would have left this place if she had the choice. Why all the attention?

Zora looked in that direction when she couldn't stand it any longer. A wiry woman with thinning hair and a mole on her cheek smirked at her. Two other women with matching tattoos on their forearms that looked like her sidekicks flanked her on either side. The woman with the mole had eyes as cold as dead fish, and she ran a finger across her tattooed throat in Zora's direction.

Zora's heart pounded against her chest, and bile rose in her mouth. She knew what the sign meant, but her best hope was to feign ignorance. Zora couldn't let the woman see her fear.

She maintained a bored facial expression, and her

eyes swept the room before returning to the table in front of her. Sandy must have seen the woman's gesture, because she swore under her breath and scrambled away from Zora as fast as she could.

The trio got up and headed in Zora's direction. The other inmates in Zora's vicinity sensed their approach, because they scattered like roaches.

Zora's heart galloped, and sweat broke out on her skin. She schooled her features, though her senses remained heightened. She adjusted her pose to make it easy for her to flee at short notice.

The group got closer… Six feet… five feet…

Zora's breath quickened. This was really happening, and it seemed the COs were doing nothing about it.

Four feet… three feet… two feet. Zora clenched her fists to prevent herself from jumping up and running.

Then a body dropped into the seat Sandy had vacated.

Zora's eyes jerked up to see who it was. Kelly! Who would have thought? She sat there examining her nails, her face mirroring the boredom that Zora had projected a few moments ago. Zora's eyes swung back to the trio, only to see they'd changed directions and were now headed to another corner of the space.

Zora let out the breath she hadn't known she'd been holding. Something about Kelly must have scared them away, since she was pretty sure they'd been heading for her. Whatever it was, she was just grateful they were gone.

She said nothing to Kelly, who did the same. But Zora wondered about Kelly's endgame. Was she offering protection for something, like maybe Zora becoming her little girlfriend? She'd heard some inmates did that. But Zora had no plans to become one, not now, not ever.

The horn sounded, which was music to Zora's ears. Kelly got up and left. Zora's eyes searched the area, but she couldn't see the trio anymore.

Her shoulders relaxed. Thank goodness she could return to her cell, which seemed like the safest place for her right now.

The COs herded them back to their cells. Zora wrapped her arms around herself and tried to avoid bumping into anyone. She'd never been so glad as when the solid steel door closed behind her. She made a beeline for her bed and collapsed on it.

Zora's limbs shook, and she hugged herself tightly. What had happened in the common area had been terrifying, yet she was certain this wasn't the end. How was she going to survive until Monday?

There was a loud banging on her cell door and Zora sat up. What was it now?

The door swung open, and a figure stood at its entrance.

Zora gasped.

12

S tewart entered the cavernous space that was the family dining room. His father was a stickler for keeping to the old traditions and loved to have all his meals served in a formal style. This was the one time his father brokered no disturbance from anyone, unless it was a dire emergency. Those who had attempted it before had ended up in watery graves.

But Stewart couldn't wait until the next day. He'd heard his father was having a late breakfast, and getting him to back off Zora's case was worth the gamble to meet him. Hopefully, his father's love for his only son would make him overlook the mistake.

His father, Anatoly Petrykin, looked up as

Stewart walked in. A frown creased his face, and he set down the newspaper he'd been reading.

It was sometimes hard to believe this was the man that had fathered him. They looked nothing alike: his father had a wrestler's profile and could be considered handsome even with his short stature and wide forehead. How his meaty hands managed to handle the tiny teacup with such dexterity had always been a marvel to Stewart until this day. Stewart, on the other hand, had taken after his mother's father and was average-statued with a bulbous nose and thin lips that marred what otherwise would have been a handsome face. His short brown hair didn't behave as well, sticking out at weird angles.

But what Stewart lacked in physical resemblance was more than made up in the intelligence that lurked behind his eyes. Stewart's mom had run away from his father when she was pregnant and had given Stewart her father's last name to avoid detection, but his father had found them both and decided his mother's influence was no longer required in young Stewart's life. She'd died a few years later. His father had opted to let Stewart keep his last name for some reason best known to him, one that Stewart didn't understand or care enough to figure out. As far as he was concerned, it was just a name.

Stewart had been his father's favorite for years, as much as anyone could be. He'd raised Stewart on the milk of violence, and Stewart had developed a keen ability to cut up body parts from a young age. Getting trained as a doctor had only been to leverage the profession's cloak of respectability while practicing the craft he enjoyed. He'd watched how his father handled the family's business, and Stewart planned to make it much more. But that could only happen when the old man was dead. Stewart was willing to wait until then—he already had a lot on his plate for now.

"What is it?" his father barked.

Tread softly, Stewart, he told himself.

Stewart strode toward his father's side and stopped a few feet short. From the corner of his eye, he could see the burly Vaslav get up from a high-backed chair stationed next to the French doors that led to the outdoor patio and move closer. It was even better the man was here—Vaslav wouldn't have the chance to convince the old man behind his back once Stewart was gone. "It's about the Smyth case," he said to his old man.

His father's eyes narrowed, and he dropped the teacup, picked up his napkin, and wiped his lips.

Not a bad sign, Stewart mused. He looked his

father in the eye, just the way the old man had taught him. "I want to handle it on my own."

"Boss, the doctor could draw unnecessary attention to our business if we're not careful," Vaslav countered. "We need to nip it in—"

His father raised his hand. Vaslav fell silent.

Stewart held back a snicker. The man would never learn. His father hated anyone interrupting his conversation with Stewart and would pay back the insolence later today.

"Why didn't you tell me about it?" his father asked Stewart.

Stewart pulled out one of the dining chairs and sat down. "I was handling it. I was the one who put her in jail as a warning to those helping her dig into the missing kidneys case."

His father said nothing and leveled his eyes at Stewart like a hawk eyeing his prey. *I'm sure he's trying to figure out what I'm thinking,* Stewart thought. After a few moments, the old man picked up his newspaper. "Okay. But there'll be consequences if you fail," his father said.

Stewart nodded. "Yes, sir." He saw the muscle in Vaslav's jaw twitch, and the corners of Stewart's lips turned up.

"Daddy!" a voice called out.

Stewart cringed. He didn't need to turn his head to know it was his so-called sister, Alisa, walking up behind him. She reached his father and kissed him on the cheek.

His father's face lit up with a smile. "Ah, Solnyshko!" *My little sun.*

Stewart's eyes darted to Vaslav, and he could practically see the drool dripping from the corner of the man's mouth.

Stewart smirked. He'd always known the guy had the hots for his sister, but his father would never allow it. Vaslav could find himself at the end of a shotgun if his father ever found out.

Alisa straightened and turned to Stewart. "Hello, Thomas," she said in a cool tone.

Stewart clenched his fists under the table. She was the only one who persisted in calling him by that name, even though she knew he hated it. "Alice," he responded. That had been her name before his father changed it to Alisa.

Stewart had been the sole darling in his father's eyes until the morning he'd woken up and seen his father talking to a little girl. He'd asked who she was, and his father had announced that she was now his little sister.

The attention Stewart had to fight for from his

father, she'd garnered with only a flick of her honey-colored hair. Now she was a practicing corporate lawyer, which made Stewart hate her more. She handled all the contracts for his father's legitimate enterprise, and the old man had ceded more control of that side of the business to her as time went by. But Stewart planned to kick her out from the family as soon as his father died. No adopted child was going to take what was his by right.

But he would tolerate her for now. The old man could have his toy until Stewart was ready.

Stewart felt something soft brush by his leg. He looked down and saw a chocolate and white furry bundle nestled at his feet.

The corners of his mouth turned up. Sparky, Alisa's one-eyed chihuahua. Alisa had rescued him from a shelter, but he'd followed Stewart religiously from the first day he'd arrived and whenever he spent the day here. Sparky was the one thing Stewart didn't mind in this house.

He bent down and scratched Sparky's back. Sparky rolled over for a belly rub.

Stewart smiled and obliged him, and Sparky wagged his tail in response.

But then it was time to leave. Stewart straightened and got up. "I have to go," he said to his father.

"Take care of it," his father replied.

Stewart nodded. He could tell from Vaslav's facial expression that he wasn't happy about the decision.

The man would not give up and would try to find a way around his father's decision.

Stewart would have to keep his eye on him.

13

Zora watched with wariness as Kelly entered the room. The cell door closed with a loud bang behind her, and Zora jumped a little. Her eyes followed Kelly as she dropped her things on the upper bed.

Kelly said nothing—she made her bed and then climbed onto it.

But what was Kelly doing here? She was the last person Zora expected to be her cellmate. Weren't convicts supposed to be in a separate wing from those awaiting trial?

Unless there was a reason for it.

Zora stilled. Only two plausible explanations came to mind: the cartel had sent her to finish the job, or she'd assumed Zora would be her little girlfriend.

Well, sorry to disappoint you, Kelly. Neither option works. She'd fight tooth and nail for her life and her reputation if it came to it.

The hourly counts came and went, but Kelly said nothing to her. Dinner was served, and the woman picked up her tray and ate in silence.

Zora forced herself to eat. She needed all her strength if there was going to be a fight for her life.

She stayed awake all night with her back against the wall, waiting for any attack, but none came. Zora was exhausted by morning, but alive.

Zora got out of bed silently to use the toilet before her roommate woke and did a courtesy flush when she was done, only to look up and see a pair of dark brown eyes staring at her.

She moved back into bed without a word. She'd planned to exercise a little, but that could wait. Who knew what Kelly would try with Zora's back turned?

Kelly relieved herself and then completed a series of squats and lunges. Zora watched and waited. She wished she could do the same, but it wasn't worth the risk.

Breakfast arrived, and they both ate. By now, Zora had gotten used to eating in the same space as the toilet and didn't even notice the smell.

Kelly sat cross-legged on the floor with her tray

on her lap. "I'm Kelly," she said, breaking the silence.

Zora said nothing and continued to eat. She didn't know what jail etiquette was regarding conversation, but it was best to err on the side of caution.

"I know your mother," Kelly said.

Zora's head flipped up in surprise.

14

Zora waited for Kelly to say more, but she didn't elaborate on what she'd meant, and now the statement played on a loop in Zora's mind as she stepped into the communal shower with its shower heads lined along the wall.

The place smelled of urine and soap, and dried soap suds dirtied the back wall of the shower room, but Zora was grateful for the chance to wash off everything that clung to her skin. There were only a few inmates using the place, Zora planned to make the shower a quick one.

She dropped her towel over one of the shower knobs and turned it on. Cold water streamed from above, and Zora basked in the feeling as it flowed over her skin and underwear. She applied the sliver of soap she'd received and rinsed off.

Then she noticed the place was now deathly quiet.

Zora looked around. She'd been so caught up in her world she hadn't realized all the other inmates were gone. An uneasy feeling enveloped her, and she turned off the shower and grabbed her towel.

Someone coughed, and Zora turned to see the tattooed woman from yesterday with her sidekicks.

Her breath caught in her throat. *God, help me.* It seemed the woman made good on her threat.

Zora had to leave now.

She wrapped the towel around her chest and tried to leave, but one sidekick blocked her way. She made another attempt, and the other sidekick pushed her back. The tattooed woman gave a vicious laugh.

Zora took a deep breath and let it out. *Stay calm, Zora.* There had to be a way out. She refused to make eye contact with either of them and made a move toward the left side again. The tattooed woman swung out at her and hit Zora's jaw.

A searing pain flashed through her head, and Zora staggered back. She shook her head to clear the fog that threatened to envelop her, but her vision was still clouded.

Hands grabbed her arms, and Zora struggled to shake them off. But the sidekicks tightened their grips.

Zora shook her head once again, and the fog cleared. She saw the tattooed woman holding a towel stretched out between her hands with an evil smirk on her lips. Zora kicked out more furiously to free herself, but she couldn't shake the sidekicks off.

The woman looped the towel around Zora's neck and squeezed. Zora struggled for air and punched one sidekick in her stomach. The woman groaned but held on.

God, please help me. She had no plans to die here. This was a fight she would not let them win. Zora kicked at the tattooed woman. The woman absorbed the punch without flinching and squeezed the towel some more.

Zora's vision clouded, but her hands clawed at anything they could touch. It must have been effective because another sidekick swore and then punched Zora's side.

She doubled over and the pressure of the towel around her neck lessened with the movement, giving Zora the window of opportunity she needed.

She drove her head with all the force she could muster into the tattooed woman's stomach.

The woman screamed, and the towel ends in her hands jerked.

Zora's little air supply got cut off, and her vision swam. She would lose consciousness if she didn't get any air soon. *God, I need your help!*

She heard a snap, and the hold around her neck loosened. Then the towel fell away from her neck.

Zora coughed as she struggled to breathe in much-needed air. *Thank you, God.* She saw through her blurred vision that the tattooed woman was now on the floor. Kelly was throwing punches at the sidekicks holding Zora's arms, and they went down. Then Zora was finally free.

Kelly pushed Zora behind her. "Stay low," she commanded.

The tattooed woman got up from the floor and wiped the blood from her mouth. "You can't stop me," she said.

"Walk away," Kelly said. Zora stayed behind her. "This is your last chance."

By now, the sidekicks had gotten up, and they exchanged glances.

The tattooed woman laughed. "No CO will come to your rescue. You are dead meat." She pulled out a sharpened toothbrush. Then she rushed forward at Kelly and Zora with her sidekicks flanking her.

What happened next was so fast Zora wasn't sure if it was real. A slim lady with long, dark hair appeared out of nowhere and stabbed the tattooed woman from behind three times. Another inmate appeared and took down the sidekicks. Blood gushed everywhere and flowed into the shower drain.

Zora froze. This couldn't be happening.

The slim lady turned to Kelly and Zora. "Leave!" she commanded.

Kelly dragged Zora by the hand toward the bathroom exit, and Zora avoided the spots where blood had pooled.

But she had to know. She turned back to the slim lady. "Why?" she asked.

The lady leveled her light brown eyes on her. "Because you are family."

15

Zora huddled on her bed, her whole body shaking like a leaf. Kelly had climbed into hers and kept quiet. But Zora couldn't stay still. The incident at the showers felt like an out-of-body experience with Zora watching from the side-lines. Sure, she'd seen patients dying in front of her, but it was nothing like this. She was not used to such brutality and violence.

She pulled her knees up and wrapped her arms around them. Was the tattooed woman dead? Zora didn't want anyone dying on her behalf, even though the woman had tried to kill her. She closed her eyes and rested her head on her knees, but she couldn't shake the image of the woman as she'd gone down from her mind.

Zora took a deep breath and exhaled. What was going to happen now? Did it mean she was an accessory to murder, even though she'd harmed no one and had only been defending herself? Zora shivered at the thought.

She recited Psalm Twenty-Three quietly, hoping it would help. It'd always had a calming effect on her whenever she'd had nightmares of her sister in the past. Soon the panic that frayed the edges of her mind melted away.

But what had the slim lady meant? Zora was not a member of any gang and wasn't trying to join one. Did it mean she now owed whoever had saved her life? What would be the price?

The hourly counts rolled by, but the COs said nothing.

Zora wondered. Hadn't they seen the body?

She waited the rest of the day, but no one came to take her away. Kelly went about her business like nothing had happened.

Zora eventually fell into a listless sleep.

———

Zora reached for her smiling sister, who stood a few feet away in a flowing golden-colored gown that enhanced her doe-like brown eyes. Zora couldn't believe she was alive and so close. Her mom would be ecstatic.

Then two dark figures grabbed her sister's arms and held her. Her sister screamed, and the sound reverberated through Zora's body, searing her heart.

Zora cried out and scrambled to grab her sister, but she couldn't reach her no matter how much she tried.

Then a larger figure appeared behind her sister and stabbed her repeatedly. Blood dripped down the front of her gown and spilled to the ground. Zora watched in horror as life drained from her sister's eyes and then she slumped.

She screamed until she couldn't.

Her eyes jerked open. Zora's pulse raced, her body a damp mess.

"Shh, shh." Zora turned her head at the sound. It was Kelly, brushing the wet tendrils of Zora's hair away from her face.

Zora's heart pounded wildly, and she scrambled away from her and huddled in the corner of her bed. "Stay away from me," she said in a hoarse voice.

Kelly backed away from the bed and leaned against the wall. "You had a nightmare."

Zora said nothing. It had been a while since she'd had one, and what happened today had triggered it.

They stayed that way for a few minutes. No COs came by, which was a relief.

Then Zora spoke. "Why did you help me?"

Kelly let out a sigh. "Because you're your mother's daughter."

"What does that mean?"

Kelly folded her arms in front of her and closed her eyes.

So she wasn't planning on telling Zora anything. But no matter who Kelly was and what she had up her sleeve, Zora understood one thing: the woman had taken an enormous risk to save her life. "Thank you," she said.

Kelly nodded. Then she pushed away from the wall and climbed into her bed.

Zora placed her head on her knees and prayed until her heart slowed to its normal pace. But she couldn't relax and stayed in that position for a few hours.

Then she fell asleep.

16

Zora's whole body ached when she woke up. It'd been a trying night, but the trauma of yesterday's event seemed to have receded somewhat.

She changed and used the toilet to freshen up, only to realize her cellmate was no longer in the room, yet Zora hadn't heard her leave. Even the COs didn't make a fuss at her absence when they conducted the regular standing count. Did that mean Kelly had their permission?

Zora's breakfast arrived, and she forced herself to eat, though the food tasted like sawdust in her mouth. Time passed, still there was no Kelly. Zora hoped she was okay, and that nothing had happened to her in relation to yesterday's events.

"Smyth, you have a visitor," the CO-on-duty called out.

Zora's heart quickened, and she felt a lightness in her chest. Maybe it was her mom—she'd promised she would come. Zora stood and waited for the CO to open the cell door and put on the handcuffs. She followed him down the hallway, and he led her to the same visiting booth she'd be in on Saturday and opened the door. The last user of the booth must have farted a lot because a rank smell hit her face, but Zora ignored it and stepped in.

Zora smiled as she saw who stood on the other side of the glass partition and gave her a small wave.

Marcus. It'd been ages since she'd seen him. They'd drifted apart over the years as they'd both concentrated on their respective careers, though they'd stayed in touch through the occasional phone call.

She was glad he'd come. It didn't matter if it was her mom or him—Zora just craved some contact with the outside world.

The CO removed her handcuffs and stepped out of the room. Zora hurried forward, sat down, and reached for the wall phone. Marcus did the same.

"Zora, are you okay?" Marcus asked, his eyes full of concern. "What happened to your face?"

Zora touched her jaw and gave him a small smile. She'd forgotten about the bruise from the punch. It seemed minuscule now in the grand scheme of things, and there was no way she was going to tell him what had happened—Marcus might go ballistic, and she couldn't afford to have him in jail as well. "It's nothing. When did you get back?" she said to change the conversation.

"Today," Marcus replied. "I took the next flight back as soon as I heard."

Warmth spread through Zora's chest. It was still nice to hear her big brother cared, even though she'd always assumed that to be the case. "I'm surprised they allowed you to see me."

"Well, I'm part of your legal team."

"Right. You are the investigator for the case."

"No, I'm one of the attorneys on the case."

Zora's eyes widened. "Since when?"

"I was admitted to the bar a few months ago."

"You didn't tell me!"

Marcus chuckled. "I'd planned to have a little get-together for everyone and break the news, but I've been traveling for work for the past few months and haven't had the chance."

Zora smiled, though it made her sad he hadn't

seen it fit to tell her as soon as it'd happened. "Congratulations!" she said.

"Thank you." Marcus leaned forward. "So, how are you doing?"

Tears pricked behind Zora's eyes, but she refused to let them fall in front of Marcus. It would break him. She inhaled instead and leaned back. "I'm fine. Any news on the case?" Her eyes searched Marcus' face.

Marcus kept his features impassive. "We're still looking for evidence to support your alibi at the time of Dr. Edwards' death. I'm sure we'll find something soon."

Zora wrapped her free arm around herself. "Unfortunately, I didn't go out that day," she said. "So there were no records of my movement on any CCTV." Then she remembered something and leaned forward.

Marcus noticed the change in demeanor and did the same. "What is it?"

"I remember signing for a package that morning, though I'm not sure if it covers Dr. Edwards' estimated time of death. A TPS courier guy delivered it."

An excited look crossed Marcus' face. "That's good news. I'll follow up on it."

Zora's heart flickered with hope. This might just

be the break she needed. She knew Marcus would pound the pavement if necessary to track the courier service employee down. "How's everyone?"

"You mean your mom? She's working hard on getting you out. She wanted to come, but I talked her out of it, since I wanted to see you. Only one attorney is allowed at this time."

Zora's shoulders relaxed. She'd been disappointed at her mom's absence and had wondered if her mom was back at missing Zora's most important moments, like she had in the past. It was good to hear that wasn't the case.

"Do you have questions?" Marcus asked.

Zora hesitated. Should she ask?

"You can go ahead," Marcus reassured her. "This conversation is not being recorded. Lexinbridge is strict about attorney-client privilege for jail communications."

"I know. My mom already told me," Zora said. *Okay, here goes nothing.* "What does it mean when someone says you are family?"

"Hmmm... I would think that means you're related."

"I know that. I mean in jail."

An unreadable expression crossed Marcus' face.

"Just ignore it. It means nothing. You have no family member in the jail system."

Zora's eyes searched his. Something told her Marcus was hiding something, but she trusted him enough to know he would tell her if it was important. She shelved the slim lady's comment for now. "Okay. So, what are my chances of making bail tomorrow?"

Confidence shone from Marcus' eyes. "I think they're good. The prosecutor is going to try to sabotage it, but we're ready. Zora, we'll do everything to get you out."

She nodded. She heard the door crank open behind her. "I think it's time to go."

"Please take care of yourself, okay?"

"I will." She got up and thrust her hands in front of her. The CO handcuffed her and then led her out of the room.

17

Marcus stepped into his SUV and shut the driver's door. He dropped his briefcase on the passenger seat beside him and leaned back into the headrest. Marcus had tried to hide it when visiting her, but he was worried about Zora.

He tugged at the navy blue tie around his neck to loosen it and ran his hands through his hair. Marcus had noticed the bruise not only on her face but also on her neck. If he had to guess, someone had harassed her or even made an attempt on her life.

Marcus pounded his fist against the steering wheel. The cartel had gone too far. He wished he could just get her out of jail this instant, but that wasn't the way things worked in the criminal justice system.

He let out a long sigh. Marcus was just glad to see her alive. She'd come out none the worse for wear—she hadn't been skittish or panicked, and he could read Zora. Uncle Jimmy's people must have done their work to protect her.

Marcus pulled out his phone and dialed the number.

Someone picked up on the other end. "Marcus."

"I just wanted to say thanks for having your people take care of Zora."

"It was nothing. Did she tell you about it?"

"She didn't. What happened?"

"I think it's best if you hear it from her, but it wasn't pretty. I'm going to dig more to find out what's going on."

Marcus sat up straight. That was the last thing he wanted. "You don't have to. We'll handle it the legal way."

Uncle Jimmy was silent for a moment. "Okay, if you say so. But reach out if you need my help. You know you are family."

"Thanks," Marcus said, and ended the call.

He slumped back on the headrest and sighed. Fine, he was grateful for his uncle's help, but that was where he drew the line. His uncle meant well, but Marcus couldn't afford any further entanglements beyond that. No good could come from it.

Because if he wasn't careful, he might pay the price with his life one day, like his father had done.

18

The CO led Zora toward the common area.

"I thought we were going back to the cell," Zora protested.

The guard didn't respond and just prodded her along. Zora had no choice but to comply. Soon they arrived at the place.

Many inmates already sat there, some playing cards, a few reading books or otherwise looking bored, while others watched a medical drama airing on the flatscreen TV. She looked around for Kelly but couldn't find her. Neither were the trio that had attacked her nor the two-person team that had saved her. It was like the incident had all been a dream.

Zora noted that the spot she'd occupied last time was vacant, so she headed in that direction and sat on the seat. Since she wasn't interested in any of the ongoing activities, Zora kept her head down and minded her own business. Her mind wandered to what had happened the last few days, trying to figure out if there were any clues that might break the case, but she stayed hypervigilant. There was no guarantee another attack wouldn't take place.

She sighed with relief when the horn sounded, announcing the end of the activity period. Thank goodness it was over—nothing had happened. Just a few more hours, and then she'd be able to make bail and leave this terrible place behind.

Zora jumped to her feet and joined the throng as they made their way out of the area. The movement slowed as they got into line. Zora folded her arms over her chest to avoid crashing into anyone.

Someone bumped against Zora, and she jumped back to minimize contact. She felt a sharp pain on her left side where the person had brushed by her, and she placed her hand there to rub away the pain. Instead, she felt a sticky fluid, and she held her hand up to look at it. It was blood, its metallic cloying scent filling her nostrils.

Someone had stabbed her just when she'd thought she was home free. The cartel had finally succeeded.

Zora's vision narrowed, and her heart pounded in

her chest as the blood continued to drip from her side onto the floor, but she fought hard against the dizziness that followed.

Soon she staggered. Zora reached to grasp something, anything, but her hand only met air. The surrounding inmates had scurried away. Not that she blamed them. No one wanted to take the rap for an attempted murder or even murder, depending on what the outcome was. But she had no plans for the latter. Zora would not let the cartel win.

She pressed her hand by her side to stop the flow of blood, though some of it still trickled past. *Zora, hang on. You can do this.* She smashed her other hand over it. *Better.* Her heart still pounded in her chest, and she inhaled deeply to draw in more oxygen.

Then her legs buckled beneath her. Zora collapsed on the floor, struggling with each breath, the pain from her side blinding her.

Then her world went black.

19

Zora opened her eyes to see Brian Atkinson, her BFF and fellow resident at Lexinbridge Regional Hospital, watching over her. Worried lines creased his forehead as he adjusted her sheets. They'd met during residency when Zora had tripped and poured coffee down his shirt and had remained friends ever since.

Zora glanced around. She was in what looked like a hospital room and they'd hooked her up to a cardiac monitor on her left.

"She's awake," she heard Brian say.

Was this a dream? She'd been in the common area at the county jail from what she recalled, and not here where Brian was.

Soon, her mom joined him, her hair swept to the

side in an haute coiffure that complemented her cream pant suit and the diamond-studded earrings in her earlobes. Silas Park, her mom's number two guy at her law firm and a well-known criminal lawyer, hovered as well, clad in his customary three-piece pinstriped power suit.

"Are you alright?" Silas asked.

Zora was definitely not dreaming.

She tried to sit up from the hospital bed she was lying in. A sharp pain pierced her side, and Zora collapsed back on the pillows. She'd forgotten about the stab wound.

"Take it easy," Brian cautioned. He adjusted the bed to elevate her head a bit.

"Thank you," Zora said with a tired voice. "Where am I?"

"At Lexinbridge Regional. Someone stabbed you," Brian said. "The COs found you in time and rushed you here right away and we got you into surgery ASAP."

Thank goodness she hadn't lost her life. She smiled at Brian. "Thank you," she said.

"You're welcome," Brian said as he returned her smile. "You were lucky—the attacker missed all the important organs."

"Because I jumped back at the last minute."

"That was smart. It saved your life."

"I didn't even realize it was an attack. I only reacted that way to minimize contact—easiest way to make an enemy over there."

"Good thinking on your behalf," Brian said. "But Zora, what happened to you? We found marks on your neck and a large bruise on your jaw. Luckily, you had no jaw fracture, but there was evidence of previous significant swelling."

That was one story Zora had no plans to tell yet. She looked at her mom, who'd moved to Zora's side and now held her hand. "An inmate attacked me the evening before, but I don't want to talk about the incident right now," Zora said.

Her mom patted her hand. "It's okay. I'm here whenever you're ready."

Zora gave her a smile. She wasn't sure she'd ever take her up on the offer, but it was nice to know her mom was available to chat. "So, what day is it? Am I going back to jail?"

"There's no way I'm going to let that happen," her mom reassured her.

Zora chuckled. Mama bear to the rescue. Her mom smiled back.

"Today is Monday," Silas said. "You've been out for about twenty-four hours. We've arranged for the initial appearance to take place at the hospital whenever you regain consciousness. I'm sure they've informed the DA's office that you're awake. The initial appearance may take place this afternoon."

Zora was onboard with having it in the hospital. The mere thought of going to the courtroom and back made her weary.

"Oh, and Stewart tried to come in and see you," Brian said. "We thought it best to restrict access beyond the normal protocol, given what has happened, and the hospital agreed with us. So the prison guards outside your room turned him away."

"You did good," Zora replied. Right now, she didn't want to see any of her colleagues, only her family and close friends.

"Why don't we let you rest for now?" Silas said. "We need to make sure the initial appearance is ready to go in the next few hours."

"Okay," Zora said, and closed her eyes. Thank goodness for wonderful family and friends.

She'd survived the attack.

Zora would get through whatever else they threw in her way.

Judge Mary Vernon, the prosecutor, and Silas were at Zora's bedside for the hospital arraignment. A court clerk was present as well, to record the proceedings. Silas stated for the record that he was appearing for Dr. Zora Smyth, who was present on the hospital bed. The atmosphere was solemn, and Zora waited with apprehension.

Judge Vernon, a buxom fair-skinned lady with streaks of gray in her dark hair, dispensed with the preliminaries, and the prosecutor—a tall thin man with a bald head and thin-veined hands—stated that Zora was charged with voluntary manslaughter. The judge asked Silas if he wanted to be heard on the motion he'd filed.

"Your Honor, we're requesting Dr. Zora Smyth's release on bail in a reasonable amount. The defendant has no criminal history, is a lifetime resident of Lexinbridge, owns a home here, has a stable work condition as a surgeon in this very hospital, and has strong ties to the community," Silas stated.

"Counsel, what's the state's position?" Judge Vernon asked the prosecutor.

"Your Honor, we ask that you deny bail. The defendant is a flight risk based on her family's wealth, and we have evidence to prove that she planned to kill Dr. Edwards."

Zora gave the prosecutor a hard stare. What evidence? It was bogus for sure.

Judge Vernon turned to Silas. "Do you have anything to add?"

"Your Honor," Silas replied, "two attempts were made to take the defendant's life since her arrest last Friday, and there is no guarantee they won't succeed next time."

It was actually three times if she included the attempt in the communal shower, but Zora said nothing. She wasn't sure how much cover-up was already in place, and she had no witnesses—Kelly and the two-woman team had disappeared.

Judge Vernon looked through the stack of papers on the hospital bed table they'd brought in for her use. "I only have one record of attempt noted here."

"Your Honor, the defendant's cellmate tried to suffocate her on Friday night," Silas said. "I have notarized witness testimony to corroborate the event took place."

Judge Vernon turned to the prosecutor. "Counsel, what's going on here? And why wasn't she placed in protective care when that happened?"

"Your Honor—"

"Bail is set at five million dollars, and the defendant is ordered to surrender her passport."

Yes! Zora's shoulders relaxed like an enormous boulder had rolled off her. She was free. The look on the prosecutor's face was enough to send her into a fit of laughter, but Zora held herself back. The judge wouldn't approve.

Now she could find out who'd framed her and who was so desperate to get her killed.

It was time to stop them.

The hunted was now the hunter.

20

Prosecutor Charles Trent gripped his briefcase as he left Dr. Smyth's hospital room. He hadn't expected the judge to grant her bail, since it was supposed to be an open-and-shut case, with the evidence he had. Charles had heard about Silas Park and done his due diligence to make sure he was ready. But Silas had one-upped him.

A muscle twitched in his jaw. Why hadn't the sheriff and his deputies told him about the other attempt on her life? There was no way they wouldn't have known about it. Why would they hide such crucial information from him? Unless there was more to the case than he knew, things that had happened in jail they didn't want him to know about. Charles had worked with them for many years, and he'd learned to turn a blind eye to whatever happened there. But he'd lost face in front of the judge because of them, and he deserved an explanation. Charles wondered what excuses the sheriff would make.

Someone bumped into him, and his briefcase crashed on the floor.

Charles cursed under his breath. He knelt down and picked up his briefcase, ready to give a piece of his mind to whoever had crashed into him. But the words died in his mouth as his eyes met the soulless black eyes that had haunted him in the past few days.

He'd grown up with a salesman father and a mom who enjoyed her role as a homemaker. Charles had vowed he'd never end up like them, content with their little white house in middle class suburbia. He, Charles, belonged to society's elite, and he saw no reason to accept any other life but that.

He'd gotten top grades and gone to the best schools, and had been on track to fulfilling his ambitions. But then an incident in college had gotten him into trouble. Charles had attended a frat party, but hadn't realized it was being used as a cover for drug distribution to college students. The cops had arrived, and without connections of his own, Charles had ended up as the fall guy, with no one to bail him out.

But an anonymous sponsor had come to his rescue, and that had been the beginning.

He'd introduced Charles to connections he'd never thought possible. Suddenly, he'd had access to all the money he needed, and ladies hung onto his words like he was a Greek god. Charles had lied and told everyone he'd come into some inheritance. He'd lived a lavish lifestyle in law school, and when he was ready to graduate, had set his sights on Lexinbridge. Charles had heard the Lexinbridge DA's office had connections to the corridors of Washington, and Lexinbridge's elite decided who filled what spots in the DA's office. Yet his sponsor had done the impossible and gotten him a job there, and all his cases had brought him one step closer to his dream.

Then, he'd gotten a call asking him to take the Zora Smyth case. It was the first request he'd gotten from his sponsor, and Charles knew not to ask questions. A man with soulless black eyes had delivered the package with the evidence and had kept tabs on him ever since. It was like the man was there anywhere he turned.

Charles had his doubts about the case. It was likely Dr. Zora Smyth was not guilty. Unfortunately, it was the good doctor's fault she'd gotten on his sponsor's bad side. Charles had no plans to do the same. If he messed up, the consequences were unimaginable—he was certain his whole life would collapse. He'd known from the beginning that nothing was ever really free, and it was time to pay for the comfort and lifestyle he'd grown accustomed to. Now he was running into issues with the case, which he couldn't afford.

"Tell me," the man commanded, his eyes fixed on Charles.

Charles shivered and got up with his briefcase in hand. He hated seeing this man, but he had no choice. "She made bail," he said.

The man said nothing and continued to stare at him.

Charles swallowed, and sweat broke out on his forehead. But he didn't look away—he couldn't let the man see his fear. "The judge granted it, despite my protests."

The man glared at him for a few moments. "I'll be in touch," he finally said. Then he turned and walked away.

Charles' knees grew weak, and he reached out his hand to the wall to steady himself. He'd made a deal with the devil, and meeting this man was part of dealing with the consequences. But he could not continue like this. He had to close this case quickly and get back to how his life was before—failure was not an option.

But first, he would deal with the sheriff's office to prevent a repeat of what had just happened. He knew just what to do.

His decision made, Charles straightened, pulled his shoulders back, and strode toward the hospital's exit.

21

S tewart was livid once he heard someone had tried to kill Zora. Since his father had rescinded his order, the only person who could have interfered was Vaslav. Apparently, he'd rejected the message to keep his nose out of Stewart's business.

It was time to teach the man a lesson, and Stewart looked forward to the result.

He relaxed in the black swivel chair in the small white-walled clinic office and blew out a long breath as he waited for the day's patients to arrive. It always amused him how patients thought he was a nice doctor. Well, he was, except while he extracted a victim's organs.

Some folks might call him a psychopath from what he'd learned in medical school, but he was just a guy with 'interesting' taste. Besides, all the people he'd removed organs from had been willing victims —they'd approached his group for loans to pay off their financial debt and had signed off their organs in exchange, though they probably hadn't read the fine print in the contracts they'd signed.

Stewart had only executed the terms of the contracts, like the businessman he was.

His mind wandered back to the brush off he'd received earlier today, and he bristled. Zora Smyth. He'd requested to see her in the hospital, and she'd denied him the chance. How dare she when her life was in his palm, and he could cut it off whenever he wanted? Now he was in this bad mood, one he couldn't seem to shake off. He needed some release, a way to punish her.

His phone rang, and he picked it up. "What is it, Erik?" he asked.

"They've released Zora Smyth on bail."

Stewart swore under his breath, and his nostrils flared. This wasn't the result he'd expected after all the money he'd sent flowing into the prosecutor's pockets, to keep him in the lifestyle he enjoyed.

Zora Smyth had to be ecstatic now, thinking she was finally free, but she didn't know he'd put a contingency plan in place to make her life more miserable on the chance they released her.

Stewart smirked at the thought of his next move. Zora was in for a big surprise. "What about what I asked you to take care of?"

"It's ready."

"Good. Release the information."

"Yes, boss."

"Anything from the background check?" Stewart had asked Erik to dig into the lives of those surrounding and helping Zora.

"There was nothing unusual about Silas Park. But there were a few calls between Marcus Tate and Jimmy Francone."

Stewart whistled. *The* Jimmy Francone? Who would have thought? Did straight-laced Zora know Marcus had ties to one of the toughest crime families in the area? He could imagine her blowing her gasket if she found out. "Find out more and keep me posted."

"Will do, boss. Also—"

"Yes, what is it?"

"Big Boss called in Vaslav and had one of his

fingers chopped off. He also placed Alexei in charge of the prostitution business." Alexei, one of his father's goons, had been with his father since the beginning and preferred to spend most of his time with the ladies—he was no threat to Stewart.

Stewart chuckled. His day just got better. That would teach Vaslav to remember his place and not mess with Stewart. Stewart had sent his father details of Vaslav's slush funds, most of which came from unreported earnings from his father's business. No one touched his father's money without permission, and the only reason Vaslav was still alive was because he'd saved his father's life once. But taking away the prostitution business from Vaslav was a colossal blow—it was one of his group's most important revenue sources. Stewart smiled as he imagined Vaslav's fury and humiliation at the loss.

"Anything else, boss?" Erik asked, bringing back Stewart's attention.

"That's it for now."

"Okay, boss."

Stewart ended the call and chuckled again. The news about Vaslav had put him in a good mood. Maybe he would celebrate tonight with another body. He'd heard a sweet young thing had just defaulted on her organ contract.

A knock sounded on the door, and a nurse poked her head in. "Dr. Stewart, the patients are ready for you."

Stewart flashed her a smile. "You can send them in."

Zora cinched her coat tighter. Her mom had brought a change of clothes for her from home, and it felt good to be back in her own T-shirt and pants. She'd insisted on leaving the hospital, since she couldn't stand being one more minute away from home. Right now, Lexinbridge Regional represented everything that had gone wrong for her, though it'd been a home base of sorts for her, first as a medical student for four years and then as a resident for an additional five years.

She'd first seen the missing patients here, and that was the case that had begun the downward spiral in which Zora now found herself. She needed to be somewhere safe, and home was the only place that came to mind.

Marcus had arrived and offered to take her home —her mom and Silas had gone back to the office— and he now walked beside her as they left the surgical floor and stepped into the elevator. Thankfully, the elevator was empty, and Zora didn't recognize any of the people who got on and left on other floors.

The elevators soon reached the lower level parking floor, and Zora and Marcus stepped out into the well-lit parking lot. Monday was usually a busy day at Lexinbridge Regional, since it was a Level 1 Trauma Center and the only one in Lexinbridge, which meant open parking spots were hard to find.

"This way," Marcus said and led Zora toward the far end corner where his black Ford SUV waited.

"How did you find a spot?" Zora asked as they approached the vehicle.

"I have my ways," Marcus replied, and winked at her.

Zora laughed. It felt good to be back with friends instead of in the dangerous world of jail life. She shivered at the memory.

"Are you cold?" Marcus asked with concern. "Hold on." He removed his jacket and looped it around Zora's shoulders.

Zora removed the jacket and handed it back to him. "No need, Marcus. I have a coat on. Thanks."

A camera flash blinded Zora, and she lifted her hand to block off her eyes. Then there was another, and then another, and soon a swarm of reporters surrounded them, their voices fighting for dominance as they jostled to thrust their microphones and cameras in Zora's face. Marcus threw his jacket over Zora, but it was already too late, with her face plastered all over the news by now. She didn't know whether to run, cry, or curl into a ball on the floor.

Marcus wrapped his arm around her and held her close as he fought his way through the crowd. Zora held onto him as tightly as she could. They reached his vehicle, and he opened the passenger door and lifted her in. Zora had the presence of mind to engage the door's lock. She could still hear the clicking of cameras as the reporters took more pictures, and then more and more. It was never-ending.

Marcus climbed into the driver's side, locked the door, and muscled the car through the crowd and past the hospital's parking exit. Soon, they were on their way out of the area.

Then Marcus blew out a long breath. "That was insane. What just happened back there?" he asked.

Zora couldn't say. It'd been a three-ring circus, with Zora as the monkey on display. How had they known she'd be there at that precise moment?

Marcus dialed a number, and it rang within the car's interior.

"Hello, Marcus." It was Zora's mom.

"Ma'am, we've run into some problem. I don't know how reporters found out about Zora, but they were waiting in the parking area." Zora had never heard her mom swear, but this was the first time. "I think it's safe to assume her home has been compromised," Marcus continued.

"I agree. Take her to the estate. I'll get a security team to meet you guys there."

"Will do." Marcus ended the call.

Zora wasn't going home after all.

———

The electronic gates swung open, and soon they were driving up a winding driveway to a large stately home that sat on manicured acres of land. This was the home Zora grew up in, though she'd been back only a few times since she'd left for medical school.

Zora and her mom had grown apart after her sister's kidnapping when Zora was in her last year of high school, and Zora had left home soon after for college and never returned. She didn't visit often, since she loved the freedom of her own space, even though their relationship had now improved.

Marcus stopped at the top of the driveway, and Zora got out of the SUV. An unfamiliar large man with cropped brown hair approached her. "Good afternoon, Dr. Smyth. I'm Jake Manson. I'll be responsible for your security here at the estate."

"Nice to meet you," Zora said, even though she hated the idea of being followed around and monitored.

"Hello, Jake," Marcus said. He'd come down and now stood next to Zora. "Good to see you again."

"You too, Marcus," Jake said.

Marcus turned to Zora. "Jake's company manages security for our firm and is the best at what he does. You'll be in safe hands."

"My team and I will be right outside," Jake said. "Mrs. Smyth has already given me a list of the folks allowed on the property, and we've already done a sweep of the house—it's clean."

"Thank you," Zora replied.

She reached the front of the house and slid her hand against the sensor on the right wall that Zora's mom had installed after her sister went missing. A beep sounded, and then the steel door opened.

Zora stepped into the large foyer. Watercolor paintings covered its walls, as were most of the walls in the rest of the house. They were her father's legacy. The painting gene had somehow skipped Zora, but her sister had dabbled in it even at her young age. Thinking about her sister didn't hurt as much as it used to, but Zora still missed her. She'd been the life of the family with her impish smile and her love for life.

As she stepped into the living room, someone in a black fall jacket and blue jeans rushed toward her and gave her a hug.

"Dave!" Zora said.

"I've missed you, Zora."

Zora snuggled deeper into his arms. She'd missed this—the warmth, comfort, and the feeling of being safe. She looked up into his eyes. "How did you get here?"

"I called your mom, and she gave me the update. Since I was already in the area, it was easy for me to arrive first. I came to the hospital yesterday and this morning, but the COs guarding your room wouldn't let me see you." Dave brushed a tendril of her hair away from her face. "How are you doing?"

Zora sighed. "As good as I can be."

There was a small cough behind her.

Oh, she'd forgotten about Marcus. Her face heated. "Dave, there's someone I need you to meet." She let go of him and turned to Marcus. "Dave, meet Marcus. He's one of my dearest friends and is like a big brother to me. Marcus, Dave is my boyfriend."

Marcus's face remained inscrutable as he stretched out his hand to Dave. "Good to meet you."

Dave shook his hand. "Likewise," he said in a cool voice.

Was it her imagination or had the temperature in the room cooled? She looked from Marcus to Dave. It was obvious they were assessing each other, like lions checking out their competition. The corners of her lips turned up at the thought.

"Why don't we sit?" Zora said and led Dave to the large brown leather sofa in the center of the living room before settling beside him. Marcus took the love seat opposite them.

Dave played with one of her hands. "Your mom said the reporters harassed you at the hospital. Are you okay?" he asked softly.

Zora stretched back against the sofa. "I don't know how they found out. Someone must have tipped them off."

"I'm guessing the same person behind the case," Dave said.

Zora sighed. "Why can't they just let me be?" she muttered.

"It's going to be okay," Marcus said. "Everything is going to be fine." He gave her an encouraging smile.

Zora gave him a small smile. "Thanks," she said, and closed her eyes.

"Are you sure you are okay?" Dave asked.

Zora squeezed his hand. "I'm just tired."

A loud ringtone pierced the air. "Excuse me," Dave said as he pulled out his phone from his jacket and looked at the screen. Zora noted a flicker of apprehension cross his face. "I need to take this," he said to Zora. "I'll be right back."

Dave got up and strode toward the kitchen. His voice faded as he shut the kitchen door behind him.

"Congratulations on the new boyfriend," Marcus said.

Zora's face heated. "Thank you."

Marcus got up. "Why don't I make a quick run to the grocery store? We both know the refrigerator is empty."

Zora chuckled. She didn't have to look to know

what Marcus said was true. Her mom hated cooking. "Thanks, that would be great."

Then she glanced in the kitchen's direction. "I wonder what Dave's call is all about," Zora muttered to herself.

She hoped it wasn't bad news.

23

"Afternoon, lieutenant," Dave said to the other person on the line.

Dave hadn't been able to find out anything useful about the case since Zora got arrested. None of his close colleagues could access the case file. He'd looked for Trevor after the prisoner transport, but Trevor had seized a leave of absence and travelled out of town.

He'd then pounded the streets for any information he could find. But no dice. Even Dave's usual confidential informants were not taking his call and had disappeared from their usual haunts. It was like someone had put out a word on the street that he was a man to be avoided.

"Dave, I need you to come in," the lieutenant said.

"Why? What is it about?"

"It's about the Zora Smyth case."

This was weird coming from the man who'd denied him access to the case file. But good news or bad, any information at this point was better than nothing.

"I'll be right there." Dave looked at his watch. "In about twenty minutes."

"Okay, see you then." The lieutenant ended the call.

Dave leaned against the black granite kitchen island. What could his lieutenant want to talk to him about? Hopefully, it wasn't a plan to further trap Zora. Dave would have to be careful.

He swung open the kitchen door and stepped back into the living room. Only Zora was there, and she had her eyes closed. She looked delicate, tired, and vulnerable.

Dave's hands fisted. He would wring the neck of the guy that had put her through this hell once he caught him.

He padded to her side and tapped her. "Hey, Zora."

Zora opened her eyes with an immediate look of

panic and her eyes scanned the area, and then relaxed. "Sorry, I didn't know I'd fallen asleep," she said as she sat up straight.

Dave's heart squeezed with pain at what she might have gone through, but he gave her a gentle smile instead. "No worries. I have to go to the station. The call was from the lieutenant, and he wants to see me."

A look of concern came into her eyes. "Is everything okay?"

"It's fine. Just some regular work. I'll be back once I'm done. Why don't you go upstairs and take a nap?"

"I'm fine." She yawned. "I'll take a shower instead. Go."

"I'll see you soon." He gave her a kiss on the forehead.

The lieutenant better have news for him.

Because Dave planned to find whoever was behind this and deal with him.

24

Zora scrubbed hard at her skin to remove the filth that remained from the jailhouse. If she had a way to launder her skin, she would have. But she couldn't seem to get rid of everything, despite how hard she scrubbed and how pink her skin turned. It was like it was tattooed on her and would never go away for the rest of her life.

She leaned against the large shower stall and ran her hands through her hair as the water streamed over her face. She didn't deserve this. All she'd done was care about her patients—the missing kidney ones—like any good doctor was supposed to do. Now she was in a race to save herself from being committed behind bars for a crime she didn't commit.

The sound of a helicopter buzzing over the house filled the air. It could only mean one thing.

The reporters had found her mom's home.

Zora didn't know whether to scream or pull her hair out. Couldn't they just leave her alone? All she wanted was a moment's peace, and they couldn't even let her have it. It didn't matter to them whether the allegations were true—she was just a juicy piece of news to them.

So far, they hadn't been able to connect her to her sister's kidnapping case, which was a good thing— the memories of that time were best kept buried.

But the constant overhead noise was a reminder that she was losing everything—her life, her career, and her privacy. They would forever label her as a murderer, even if she turned out not guilty.

Zora let out a tremulous breath and wiped the water from her face. She would not cry—the perp wouldn't get that satisfaction. Zora was a fighter, and whoever was behind this would not have her life that easily. It didn't matter how connected they were or how much they tried to ruin her.

She wouldn't give up.

Zora only had one choice: to reclaim her life.

It was time.

25

Dave knocked on the door of the lieutenant's office. He heard a muffled "come in" and opened the door.

Lieutenant Bandy looked up from the report he was reading at his desk and waved Dave in. The office was spacious, but the lieutenant made it appear tiny with the mountain of paperwork that overflowed from the desk and the stacks of books that stood like large chess pieces on the floor. A strong smell of fresh cinnamon donuts jostled for attention against that of day-old pizza. The lieutenant must have been at it again—the man could never let food pass him by.

Another man in a sharp gray suit that Dave didn't recognize sat in a visitors' chair facing the desk.

"I'll come back some other time," Dave said.

"No, no, come in." Lieutenant Bandy beckoned him. "It won't take long."

Dave strode in and pulled back the empty visitors' chair before sitting down.

"Okay, let's make this quick," Lieutenant Bandy said.

"So, Detective McKesson, we have on record here that you've been derelict in your duties," the unknown man, who sported a handlebar mustache, said.

Dave swung his head to look at the man. "Who are you?" he asked.

"Internal Affairs," the man replied.

He should have known. No detective out on the streets would wear such a stiff suit and shiny Italian boots.

Now everything made sense.

Dave had nursed a tiny hope that his lieutenant had changed his mind about the case, but it seemed the man was hell-bent on making sure Dave was out of the picture. But coming up with bogus charges was a low blow, even for him.

"So, what are you guys speculating that I did wrong?" Dave asked.

"Dave—"

"It's Detective McKesson," Dave corrected Lieutenant Bandy.

Lieutenant Bandy leaned back in his brown swivel chair. "Don't make this hard," he said.

"Hard?" Dave said and scoffed. "That's what I should say to you, Lieutenant."

"Look, Detective McKesson, you were unaccounted for when the station needed you to arrest Dr. Zora Smyth," the IA man said.

Dave turned furious eyes at the lieutenant. "Is that the story you fed him?" Dave said. "And while we're on the topic, is that why you gave Trevor, who has been my partner for four years, a new partner without telling me?"

Lieutenant Bandy leaned forward. "Cut it out, Detective," he responded.

"As I was saying, you were unavailable," the IA man said.

"For the record, the lieutenant asked me to track down a certain informant, and approved my time off for the rest of the afternoon once I was done," Dave responded.

"I did no such thing, Detective," the lieutenant shot back.

A muscle in Dave's jaw twitched, and he shook

his head in disbelief. He still had a hard time believing that his own lieutenant was setting him up.

"Well, Detective McKesson, you're suspended from this moment on," the IA man said. "Please hand over your badge and gun."

Dave removed his gun from his holster and dropped both it and his badge on the desk. "Thanks for the setup, Lieutenant, but it's not over. Tell the man behind you we'll get him," Dave said and then headed toward the door.

"Hey! Stop that—"

Dave slammed the door behind him and leaned against it for a moment. He'd had high hopes, but the lieutenant had disappointed him yet again. But he was in for a surprise if he thought taking away Dave's badge and gun would stop him.

Dave was going to find out the truth, no matter what it took.

26

Zora got dressed and waited in the living room for the rest of her team to arrive. She'd called them on the house phone as soon as she'd finished her shower. Thank goodness it was a private line, so the press hadn't gotten hold of it yet. Otherwise she would have had to disconnect it, and then she wouldn't have had any way to contact them. Marcus was in the kitchen putting away the groceries, and Dave had said he was on his way back. Silas had said he'd dial in via conference call. Zora had also called Christina, and she'd confirmed she was already at the airport.

The doorbell chimed, and Zora checked the security camera. It was Christina. She pressed the door release button, and Christina bounced in, her fiery red hair in a ponytail swinging behind her.

"Zora!" she cried out and dropped her bags before pulling Zora into a hug.

Tears came to Zora's eyes, and she hugged her back. "I've missed you," she said.

"I didn't know," Christina said. "You should have asked Marcus or Dave to call me. I heard about it on the news and took the next flight in. I'm so sorry for not being here for you." Christina had been at her mom's place.

"But you're here now. That's the most important thing. And it's not your fault, young lady. Come, let's sit." Zora led her to the sofa.

Christina sat down. "What's with the hunks outside?"

Zora chuckled. "My new security team." She wagged a finger at Christina. "You're not allowed to flirt with them."

"Hey, what do you take me for?" Christina said in mock annoyance. Then her face turned serious. "So how are you?" she asked, her eyes searching Zora's face. "You've lost some weight."

"I'm fine," Zora reassured her with a smile. "How is your mom?"

"She's good. Don't worry, she is going on a cruise with her best friend."

"I'm glad to hear she's doing okay."

"So, what can I do to help?" Christina asked.

"Let's wait for the others to come in, and then we can talk about it."

"Okay. Let me put away my bags in the meantime. Where am I going to sleep? Because I'm staying with you. I'm not letting you out of my sight," Christina said.

Zora chuckled. "I'll show you the bedroom next to mine."

Christina shook her head. "Not good enough. We're going to stay in the same room where I can see you. Don't worry, it will be like old times, us girls together."

Zora hugged her again. "I'm glad you're here."

Christina hugged her back. "What are best friends for?" Then she pulled away. "So, where's the bedroom?"

"It's the last one on the left when you climb up the stairs to the second floor."

"Awesome. I'll be right back." She got up, grabbed her bags, and headed up the stairs.

Zora let her head fall back on the sofa. She was feeling better already. Christina had been her best friend since high school, and they've been room-mates for the past few years. She'd stayed with her mom for a while after the kidnapping ordeal she'd suffered with Zora. It was great to have her by her side.

Christina appeared at the head of the stairs as Marcus stepped back into the living room with a glass of orange juice in his hand.

"Hey you," Christina said as she sashayed her way down the stairs. "I didn't know you were back. I thought you were out of the country."

"Hello, Christina," Marcus said. "I just got back a few days ago."

Christina grabbed the glass of juice and gulped it down. "Thanks for the drink. I needed that."

"Hey! That was for Zora," Marcus protested.

"Well, you can make her another one, or better still, brew a cup of her favorite coffee, which I'm sure is what Zora would prefer."

"Really?" Marcus looked at Zora for confirmation. Zora nodded.

"See? I told you," Christina said and handed the glass back to Marcus. "Thank you."

Zora laughed. "Christina, don't be naughty." She turned to Marcus. "Thank you. I hope it's not a bother."

"No worries. Anything for you," Marcus said, and headed back to the kitchen.

"Ooh!" Christina said.

Zora chuckled and shook her head. "Oh, cut it out," she said to Christina. Christina would never change. Zora knew she was doing all this to distract her from the ordeal she'd been through.

"So, who else are we missing?" Christina asked.

"Only Dave. We'll call Silas once we're ready."

The doorbell chimed. "That must be him," Zora said as she got up to buzz the door open.

Dave entered the living room and gave Zora a hug. His woody, spicy smell enveloped her, and she leaned in for more of his touch. Safe—that was how she felt in his arms, and she didn't want to leave.

He turned to Christina. "Hello, Christina."

"Nice to see you again, Dave. Looking handsome as always."

Zora let go of Dave. She had to agree with Christina. Lean-built with no extra fat, Dave was a sight for sore eyes. His beautiful brown eyes always drew her in, and his gorgeous dimples showed up whenever he smiled.

"I see you haven't changed," Dave said to Christina.

"Why would I?" Christina said, her green eyes

twinkling as she leaned back on the sofa. "I'm one-of-a-kind."

Dave chuckled. "That I agree with."

"What happened with the lieutenant?" Zora asked Dave.

"Just some administrative stuff. Nothing for you to worry about," Dave responded.

Dave was definitely holding back. Whatever had happened had been a big deal to him, and Zora hoped he'd eventually tell her what it was. It couldn't be easy for Dave working with colleagues who'd betrayed him.

Marcus strode into the living room at the moment with a mug in his hand. "Here you go," he said to Zora as he extended the cup to her. "You're back," he said to Dave.

"Thank you," Zora responded with a smile. Dave acknowledged Marcus with a nod and held onto Zora's free hand.

"Okay, now we can get started since we're all here," Zora said. "Just grab whatever seat you like. I'll call Silas now."

Marcus sat next to Christina, while Zora and Dave sat on the smaller couch opposite them.

Zora dialed Silas' number on the cordless home phone. "Hello, Silas. It's Zora. Is this a good time?"

"Absolutely," Silas responded from the other end of the line.

"Great. I have Dave, Marcus, and Christina here with me. Let me put you on speaker." Zora pressed the speaker phone button and placed the phone on the large round coffee table.

The front door clicked, and Zora looked in that direction. Who could it be? She wasn't expecting anyone. Though an intruder wouldn't have gotten past Jake and his team, Zora still stood up.

"What is it?" Dave asked with concern.

"Someone just entered the house, and I'm not expecting anyone."

Dave jumped up. "Let me check." He strode across the living room and then stopped.

Zora's mom came into view in her usual pant suit with a lady's briefcase and a shopping bag in hand.

Zora's eyes widened. "Mom! What are you doing here?" she asked. She'd never seen or heard of her mom clocking in less than a full day at work.

"Where else would I be?" Zora's mom said to her. She looked around the room. "I see you guys are already here."

Marcus got to his feet. "Hello, ma'am."

"Hello, Mrs. Smyth," Dave said.

Christina rushed toward Zora's mom and gave her a big hug. "Hello, mom."

A soft look filled her mom's face as she looked down at Christina. "How are you? Are you doing okay?"

"I'm good. My mom sends her regards."

"Tell her I said thank you when next you see her."

"I will." Christina let go of Zora's mom.

"Why don't we get back to the meeting?" her mom said. "Silas told me about it. I'm assuming he's on speaker?"

"Yes," Zora replied. "Silas, are you still there?"

"Yes, I am."

"Everyone, sit." Zora's mom said and placed her briefcase and shopping bag on the coffee table. She then grabbed an available chair.

"Mom, aren't you supposed to be at work?" Zora asked.

"This is the only work I have. I've cleared my schedule until your case is resolved. All that work means nothing if I can't even fight for you."

Warmth spread through Zora's chest. Her mom probably had no idea how much hearing those words meant to her.

Zora smiled at her. "Okay. Let's talk through the case." Zora shared all she remembered from the time the cops had showed up at her apartment until she'd ended in the holding cell. "I got the sense that someone was giving the orders from the shadows," Zora finished.

"I agree," Dave said. "My partner betrayed me, and my lieutenant stonewalled me. That's a big deal from two people who have never treated me that way before. My first guess would be the cartel in the organ trafficking business. They fit the profile, and they're the only ones with a beef against you. And they were Dr. Edwards' business partner."

"I would ordinarily agree," Silas said from over the speaker phone. "But I've heard a few things about the head of that East European cartel, and this is not his typical modus operandi."

"Unless there is someone else in their organization who is engineering everything, maybe a rising star," Zora's mom replied.

"But we have no evidence," Marcus said. "And the prosecutor is keeping the ones he has close to his chest for now."

"We do have some information," Silas said. "I found out from a source in the DA's office that the prosecutor has Zora's fingerprints on the scalpel that killed Dr. Edwards."

Zora's heart quickened. "That's not possible," she

said. "I never handle a scalpel without gloves. That's Gross Anatomy 101."

"Which means the fingerprints must have been planted," Marcus responded.

"Is there any way we can disprove it?" Zora asked.

"We can run an independent forensic examination on it, but we'll need access to the weapon in question. That's not possible until pretrial discovery, which won't happen until the prosecutor is ready to take it to trial," her mom said. "I'm not sure we want the case to advance to that stage if we can help it. It'll be better to get the charges dropped now."

"Okay. Silas, was there anything else?"

"They also have a witness who testified he saw Zora leaving Dr. Edwards' house at the time of the incident, though there is no CCTV to confirm it," Silas continued.

"That's just bogus!" Zora cried out. "I didn't even go out that day." Good thing she had never gone to Dr. Edwards' house before—she had no idea where he lived.

"The witness must have been paid off," Zora's mom said thoughtfully.

"I agree, and we need to track him down," Dave said. "Silas, do you have any information on him?"

"No," Silas said. "But I'll see what I can find out."

"That'll be great if you can," Zora said. "Marcus, did you find the courier guy I told you about that delivered a package to my apartment that day?"

"I tracked down the TPS employee that delivered packages to your building that day, but his office said he took a vacation that Friday, and they haven't seen him since," Marcus said. "The log for that day and any electronic information on the package, including your signature for it, is also missing."

Zora's heart sank. It was possible the enemy had scared the courier guy off.

"I found the empty package in your apartment, which is evidence enough that the courier delivered to your apartment that day," her mom said. "But there was no timestamp on it."

"I'll keep looking for the guy to see whether I can track him down," Marcus finished.

"Thank you," Zora said. "Anything else?"

"I've been looking into the CCTVs around your apartment that show the entries and exits into your building for the day," Dave said. "I've found nothing so far. Two of your building's cameras are missing videos for that day. The last one seems to have corrupted data, but one of my guys is working on it to see if he can restore some of it, though he believes it might be difficult."

Zora sighed. That didn't sound promising.

"So, what do we do now?" Christina asked.

"I think we should start from the beginning, with the missing patients' case. I don't know why, but I've always felt like the person responsible knows me well," Zora said. "But I can't think of anyone around me who bears me any ill will."

"The same way we never thought Dr. Edwards would be an enemy, but look what happened," Christina countered. "All I know is that whoever is the boss speaks Russian fluently from the conversations I overheard while I was kidnapped."

"Graham, who fled to Dubai because of the case, was the only one who I knew who spoke the language," Zora said. "And he's clearly not the person."

"Stewart speaks it too," Christina countered.

"Stewart, my resident?" Zora laughed. "He can't be the one. The guy is even afraid of his own feet!"

"Looks can be deceptive," Dave said. "I remember what Brian said about him at the hospital when you woke up after the kidnapping—I overheard it from outside the door. I believe it was 'Strange little fella. Too smooth if you ask me.' Or something like that."

"Nah, it can't be him. Let's forget it," Zora said. "Anything else?"

"That's all I have. But I'll keep my nose to the ground," Silas said. "We'll have more access in discovery, but that may be some time ahead. I have heard nothing about the prosecutor's next steps, but I'll let you know once I do."

"I'll work my networks to see if I can get some info on that," her mom said.

Zora turned to her mom. "I hope this fiasco hasn't affected the firm."

"Business is booming in the criminal practice," Silas responded over the speakerphone. "We've had lots of new clients. It's like your case gave them the stamp of approval they needed."

"It doesn't matter even if it harms the firm," her mom said. "We could always start over again."

Zora smiled. "Thanks, Mom, for saying that. Silas, please keep doing what you are doing." She turned to Dave and Marcus. "Could you please work together on finding out more about the witness?"

"We don't need to work together. I prefer to work alone," Dave said.

"Me too," Marcus countered.

Zora let out a sigh. What was it about guys and trying to prove their macho around ladies?

"Don't worry, Zora," Marcus said. "We'll share any information we have. Right, Dave?" Dave nodded in acknowledgment.

"Thanks, guys. Unfortunately, I'm stuck here, so there's little I can do."

"I'll be right here with you," Christina said.

"No worries. We've got you," Dave said. "We'll make sure nothing happens to you."

"Everything is going to be alright. I promise," her mom said.

"Zora, hang in there," Silas said. "I have to go. Talk to you later."

"Thanks, Silas, everyone." Zora ended the call and leaned back on the couch.

Her mom got up and pushed the shopping bag in her direction. "Zora, these are your personal items from the jail."

Zora grabbed the bag and pulled out her phone. "Thanks, Mom." She waved her phone. "I've missed this." She powered it on. Thank goodness it still had some juice left. Her mom most likely had a spare charger somewhere in the house, and she would look for it later. There were lots of missed calls, but none Zora was interested in returning.

Dave touched her arm. "I have to go. The sooner we work on this, the better."

"Same here," Marcus said and got up.

"Hang in there, babe," Dave said as he held her hand in his. "Everything will get better."

Zora smiled at him. "Sorry for the ruined lunch date that never happened."

"Don't worry about it," Dave said. "There will be lots of time for that in the future." He gave Zora a kiss on her forehead.

Zora prayed that was true.

Because she had no plans to return to jail.

27

Marcus gave a quick nod to the security detail standing near the entrance and strolled to where he'd left his SUV in front of Zora's mom's house. He could no longer hear the news helicopter circulating over the house—they must have gotten tired and left.

Truth be told, he was worried about Zora. She'd seemed in fine spirits a few minutes ago, but he could tell from the look in her eyes she was doing her best to hold it together. It was like the experience had taken away some of her innocence forever, replacing it with wariness.

His phone rang. Marcus stopped, pulled out his phone from his pants pocket, and looked at the screen. It was Uncle Jimmy.

Marcus let out a long sigh. Why was he calling? It wasn't like they still had any outstanding business between them. He swiped the answer button. "Hello."

"Marcus, I heard Zora got stabbed. How is she doing?"

Of course, he'd heard about it. "She's fine and is out of the hospital."

"I'm sorry that happened on our watch. But don't worry about the perp. We'll find him and take care of him."

Marcus didn't even want to know. He needed to stay in the dark about such matters. He noticed Dave looking at him from a few feet away. "Hold on," he said to Uncle Jimmy. He strode to his vehicle and got in. "Go on," he said.

"Marcus, someone has to pay for this. Whoever stabbed Zora has just declared war."

Marcus stilled. "Uncle Jimmy, please stay out of it."

"I'm sorry, Marcus, but it's too late. I'm already on it. This bastard has hurt my family. If word gets out on the street about this, it'll hurt my reputation. I can't let it go. Family is everything."

"Please, Uncle, just stop. I don't want what happened to Papa to happen again."

The line went silent for a moment. Marcus knew

the reminder had hurt him. "I'm sorry, Marcus," Uncle Jimmy finally said. The line went dead.

Marcus ran his hands through his hair. This was what he'd hoped to avoid. Who knew what the ripple effect would be?

He banged his fist on the steering wheel. Why couldn't Uncle Jimmy let things be? It was like his parents all over again.

Marcus leaned his head back on the headrest and sighed. Uncle Jimmy never changed his mind once he'd decided on something. There was nothing Marcus could do now, except put it out of his mind and focus on what he could do for Zora.

Hopefully, they'd all make it out of this nightmare okay.

He started his vehicle and drove away.

28

"**I** know you wanted more than the peck," Christina teased.

Zora's face heated. "I don't know what you're talking about."

"Oh, yes, you do. I watched how your eyes were following your man. It was like you wanted to gobble him up."

Zora threw a cushioned pillow at Christina's head. She dodged and laughed.

"I don't blame you," Christina said. "Dave is just my friend, and I even think he's hot."

"Christina, will you stop?" Zora said in mock exasperation.

Christina laughed. "I'll think about it."

Zora tensed and grabbed her side. "Ouch."

Christina drew close, a look of concern on her face. "Are you okay? Does it still hurt a lot?"

Zora grabbed Christina by the collar and ruffled her hair. Christina's familiar soft lilac scent filled her nostrils.

"Stop it, Zora. You know how much I hate having my hair messed up," Christina protested.

Zora chuckled and released her. "That will teach you to put a lock on your mouth."

"I'm just letting it go because you're a patient. But did you notice how Dave and Marcus were sizing each other up? Like you were the meat they both wanted for lunch."

Zora laughed. "Oh, please. It wasn't like that." Christina could be crazy sometimes, but she loved her just the same.

"Does Dave know Marcus is your ex-boyfriend?" Christina asked.

"Technically, we didn't start a relationship. We only dated a few times."

"I'm sure that's not what Marcus thinks."

"Marcus is dear to my heart, like a brother, but Dave is my boyfriend. I'm pretty sure I've done nothing to create any other impression beyond that."

Her thoughts turned back to the case. Zora prayed they'd both be successful in helping her make this case go away.

She jumped to her feet. "I think I need more coffee. Do you want some?"

"Let me make it for you."

"No, thanks. I need something to do."

———

Zora entered the kitchen to see her mom fiddling with the coffeemaker on the large, black granite island in the center of the room. The smell of fresh coffee and garlic bread hung heavy in the air.

"Yergacheffe coffee is still your favorite, right?" her mom asked.

Zora's eyes widened. How did she know? Zora hadn't started drinking the Ethiopian coffee religiously until college, and she'd only ever brewed it in her own place. "Yes," she said.

Her mom filled a mug with the fresh coffee and handed it to Zora.

"Thank you," Zora said, and sat on one of the kitchen stools with her hands around the mug.

Her mom moved over to the kitchen sink to wash some dishes. It was hard to believe this was the same woman that was head of one of the leading law firms in the city.

"Do you know someone named Kelly?" Zora suddenly asked. She noticed her mom's hands stilled before she continued washing the plate in her hand like nothing had happened.

"Kelly? Why do you ask?" her mom replied without turning.

"I met her in jail. She mentioned she knew you."

"I knew a certain Kelly a long time ago." Her mom said nothing else.

The ensuing silence in the room was deafening. Zora wondered what Kelly's relationship with her mom was. It was obvious there was more between them, but it was clear this was all her mom planned to say. Besides, Zora and her mom didn't have the kind of relationship where Zora could push for more answers.

Zora got up. "Thanks for the coffee," she said. She took her mug and headed back to the living room.

As she returned to where Christina sat, her phone rang. Zora pulled it from her jeans pocket.

Her heart raced as she answered the call. "This is Dr. Zora Smyth," she said.

Zora's face paled at the words she heard next.

The mug slipped from her hands and crashed on the floor.

29

"Zora, what is it?" Christina asked, panic written all over her face.

Zora swallowed. She hadn't imagined it would get worse so soon. "The hospital has fired me. Just like that."

Christina's face fell. "I'm so sorry," she said.

Zora collapsed on the couch and rubbed her eyes. "I can't believe it. How could they? This is my last year of residency, and I'm just a few months away from completing the program."

"Did they tell you why?"

"Something about it being employment-at-will, as stated in the employee contract."

"I'm sorry."

Zora ran her hands through her dark, wavy hair.

Nothing she'd gone through so far had hurt as much as this.

Her life as a surgeon meant everything to her. She'd just gone through an ordeal to get her career back a few weeks ago. Now, she'd lost it again, and it was no use taking it up with the hospital's leadership. They'd made it clear their decision was final.

Getting another residency spot in another hospital's program was out of the question—it was as rare as finding a black opal on the street. Even if she found one, they would want to know what made her leave Lexington in the first place, and the truth meant an automatic rejection. Losing her spot was like being branded with a scarlet letter.

It had to be the recent publicity that had put the nail on the coffin, and Zora cursed the perp that had set her up under her breath. Was it bad that she wished the guy could shrivel up and die?

Tears welled up behind Zora's eyes. What was she going to do now? *Get it together, Zora.* It wasn't over until it was truly over. The tide could still turn in her favor. All the efforts everyone was putting in now to find the truth would not be in vain.

Zora inhaled deeply and exhaled. This was such a hard blow to take. But her life was not over, and God had the final say. *God, I need you.*

She closed her eyes and prayed for strength. After a few moments, she felt peace calm her heart, something she needed in the days ahead. *Thank you, God.*

"Zora?" Christina asked with concern. "Are you okay?"

Zora opened her eyes and gave her a small smile. "I'm going to be," she responded.

"Okay."

"I think I'm going to turn in for the night."

Christina gave Zora a worried look. "Isn't it too early? It's barely four p.m."

"It's fine." She gave Christina a lopsided smile. "The last few days have been exhausting, and a patient needs rest to heal."

"If you say so."

Zora got up and climbed the stairs. She would rest for tonight.

Hopefully, there'd be better news tomorrow.

30

Stewart stared at the carnage on the operating table in front of him. The pungent smell of roasted flesh filled the air. He'd been in a good mood when he'd started with this victim and had only planned to remove the girl's kidneys and heart and send them to the buyers as agreed. But knowing Zora was no longer in his grasp had drowned out his glee at Vaslav's demise, and he'd wreaked havoc on the body instead. He'd ended up with no painting and no products for his customers.

All because of Zora.

He couldn't tell when she'd permeated his heart and soul. It had all started as a game, but now it seemed he couldn't do without her in his control.

Zora wasn't the first woman he'd ever been interested in; the others had been mere toys, and he'd tossed them away or even sold their organs when he tired of them. But Zora was different, and somehow she was as slippery as wet soap. Now she'd even affected his enjoyment of his daily ritual.

He swore under his breath and threw away the bloodied forceps in his hand. It knocked down an instruments bowl before clattering on the floor, leaving behind a streak of blood in its wake.

Stewart had to do something. He needed a release from the tension that had built up inside him to deliver the products on time as promised.

He pressed the call button on the wall and then removed the stained surgical garb and gloves and dumped them in the chute that led to the incinerator. Erik would dispose of the girl's body as usual.

For now, Stewart would go to his trophy room where he kept a souvenir from every body he'd ever touched. It always calmed him down when everything else failed.

But it was time to speed things up and regain control of Zora.

31

Zora woke up the next morning refreshed. Shards of sunlight edged their way in from between the closed curtains. It felt good sleeping on a bed that wasn't full of lumps and bed bugs. Christina had ended up in the guest bedroom next door, and Zora bet she was still fast asleep.

She got up and strode to the windows to take a peek outside. There were no helicopters buzzing in the air, and Zora was grateful for the uninterrupted peace.

She'd slept until about two a.m. when she'd gotten up and gone in search of water. Zora had chuckled when she found Christina dead to the world in the guest bedroom. She'd passed by her mom's home office and seen her engrossed in some files she was reading at her desk. Zora had watched her for a few moments and then returned to bed without disturbing her. She wasn't sure her mom had gotten any sleep.

Zora turned to head to the bathroom, and that was when she noticed the vase of flowers on the bedside table. It was a mix of bright-yellow spray roses, daisy pompon, and pale-yellow roses, a bouquet meant to brighten up her day, and she knew who'd sent them.

She inhaled the scents from the cheery flowers and then headed to the bathroom to wash up before making her way down the stairs. Her mom and Silas stood in the middle of the living room, talking in animated tones. They fell silent as soon as they saw her.

"Good morning," Zora said. "What's going on?"

Her mom and Silas said nothing at first. Then Silas said to her mom, "She has to know, Adrianna."

This was new. Zora had never seen Silas call her mom by her first name that way, like they had something special between them. Zora didn't mind since Silas was a confirmed bachelor and her mom was a widow. She was more surprised that nothing had happened between them all these years, considering how much time they spent together for work. But that wasn't what was important now.

"What is it?" she asked, looking from her mom to Silas.

Her mom ran her hand over her hair. "The prosecutor convened a grand jury early this morning," she said.

"And they've indicted you for voluntary manslaughter," Silas continued. "The case is going to trial."

Zora rubbed her forehead. She'd known this was a possibility, but having it become a reality was not the same. She hadn't expected it to happen so fast. Her mom reached for her, but Zora stopped her. "Give me a moment," she said. "I'll be fine."

She took a deep breath and forced herself to calm down. *It's not the end of the world,* she thought to herself. Zora moved over to the sofa and sat down. She closed her eyes for a moment and then opened them. "Do we have a date for the trial?" she asked.

"It's in two weeks," Silas replied.

So soon. Would there be enough time to crack the case? She wasn't sure.

"And a Judge Truman got the case," he continued.

They could still turn things around. "What do we know about him?" Zora asked. Her mom blew out a sigh. "What is it?" It couldn't get worse, right? "Tell me."

"The judge and I have an unpleasant history, and we've tried to avoid each other over the years," her mom said. "But he's taking this one."

Zora rubbed an eyebrow. "Is there any way to get him off the case?" she asked.

"I've already asked him to recuse himself, but he's refused. The information about the indictment and the judge for the case is already all over the news, like someone wanted to make sure changing him would be difficult."

Zora didn't know whether to cry or laugh. *Not again*. The news release had the perp's signature all over it. When would he stop and get out of her life? She ran her hands through her hair.

Zora's mom came over, sat beside her, and held her hand. "I'll not let anything happen to you, no matter what."

Silas sat on the couch opposite them. "The good news is that we'll now have access to their documents and evidence during the discovery," he said.

"But isn't two weeks too short?" Zora asked.

"We can make it work. I tried to get the judge to extend the time, but he insisted two weeks was more than enough for us to get our ducks in a row. But he's already asked the prosecutor to hand over the documents to us by tomorrow," Silas responded.

"I've heard prosecutors can give you boxes and boxes of irrelevant information just to derail you," Zora said in a worried tone.

"Don't worry about that," her mom responded, and gave her a reassuring smile. "We have more than enough manpower at the firm waiting to go through them."

Silas pulled out his phone and called a number. "Let's find out what Marcus and Dave have. We had them camp outside the courtroom as soon as we heard about the grand jury. We confirmed from an inside source that the witness was present today for it, so Marcus and Dave are now tracking him as we speak."

Zora perked up. This was good news.

Silas pressed the speaker button. "Hello, Marcus. I'm assuming Dave is with you?"

"Yes, he is," Marcus replied.

"Do you guys have anything?" Silas asked.

"We caught a picture of the individual on camera, despite how much she tried to hide her face."

"It's a 'she'?"

Zora's eyes widened. *Interesting.*

"Yes. Dave is going to send you the picture right now."

A moment later, her mom's and Silas' phones beeped.

Her mom pulled out her phone, opened the screen, and showed the picture to Zora.

Zora gasped.

32

"What's wrong?" Zora's mom asked.

"I know this woman," Zora said excitedly as she pointed at the picture. "She's from the surgical team that disappeared in the missing kidneys case." She gave her mom a questioning look. "Shouldn't we send this information to the cops?"

"Hello, Zora," Marcus said. "I don't think that's a good idea."

"I agree," her mom said. "The cops have to be on the take regarding this case, and we want nothing getting back to the criminal behind this. No offense, Dave."

"None taken," Dave said. "Hello, beautiful. That was for Zora, by the way."

Zora chuckled at his words. "Hi, guys. Dave, for a moment there, I wondered if you were hitting on my mom."

"My apologies, Mrs. Smyth. No offense," Dave said.

Her mom smiled. "I see what you did there. None taken." Her face became serious again. "So what's the plan?"

"We're going to keep following her to see who she meets and where she goes," Marcus said. "Maybe she'll lead us to the person behind everything or to some clue about his identity."

"Sounds good," Zora replied.

"She's on the move again," Marcus said. "We have to go. Zora, hang in there."

"Thanks, guys. Dave, thanks for the flowers."

"You're welcome. I hope you like them."

"I do. Thank you. I'll talk to you later."

"Sure," Dave responded. The line disconnected.

Zora's mom squeezed her hand and smiled at her. "See, we have a breakthrough already. It can only get better from here."

Zora nodded. Yes, she was grateful for the new information. But it wasn't enough, and they only had two weeks.

She prayed for a divine intervention.

Because that was what she needed now.

33

A man sat in his car and watched Marcus and Dave as they staked out in their car close to a run-down store in a shady neighborhood on the outskirts of Lexinbridge. Most of the houses in the area were dilapidated, mere shadows of a prosperous era that was long gone. They were now filled with trash, hood rats, and drug paraphernalia. He'd seen a woman in a black hooded jacket enter the convenience store a few minutes ago, and she hadn't come out yet.

He'd been tailing Marcus as ordered by the boss, and they'd ended up here. The man could bet his arm that Marcus and Dave didn't know the East European cartel ruled this territory, and staying here long enough could get them killed.

The man picked up his phone and dialed a number.

"What is it?" the gravelly voice of Uncle Jimmy asked as he answered the call.

"Boss, Marcus just found the witness in the case," the man said. "I'm sending a picture now." The man selected an image he'd snapped on his phone as the woman was entering the store and sent it across.

"Ah, a member of the East European cartel. I thought as much," Uncle Jimmy said. "This storefront is one of theirs."

"What do you want me to do, boss?"

"Keep an eye on her. Send some boys to find out what that gang is up to. I want to know what they're planning next."

"Will do, Boss."

Then the man heard the unmistakable click.

He spun in the direction of the sound while reaching for his gun, only to see one with a silencer pointed at him outside his driver's window.

That was the last thing he saw before the gun went off.

34

"Did you hear that sound?" Dave asked Marcus, his eyes alert as he peered out at their surroundings through the passenger window. Marcus had insisted they take his SUV from the courthouse, and Dave had acquiesced. It wasn't such a big deal, since Marcus was a former private investigator experienced in close surveillance.

"What sound?" Marcus asked as he popped another mint into his mouth. The guy sure loved his mints and had run through many packs since they'd started tailing the supposed witness.

"I think it was a gunshot," Dave said.

Marcus glanced at him sharply. "Where?"

Dave looked in the direction he'd heard the shot, and Marcus' eyes followed his.

"Isn't that someone slumped in that black car?" Marcus asked. He pointed to the vehicle in question.

Dave leaned forward to get a closer look. He thought he saw what was blood dripping from the side of the man's head. It looked like a one-shot-one-kill.

The hair on his skin rose. "Marcus, start the engine."

"Why?"

"Just start it!"

Marcus complied. "What now?"

And then Dave heard the sound, one he'd become acquainted with many years ago, and which had haunted his dreams in the beginning. "Go, go, go!"

The SUV's windscreen shattered, and glass rained all the backseat. Marcus didn't need any additional prompting. He hit the accelerator and hightailed it out of the neighborhood.

Dave held his breath until they were back on the highway and headed back to Lexinbridge downtown.

"What just happened back there?" Marcus asked.

Dave exhaled. "Well, Zora would have had to bury us if we'd stayed a moment longer."

"I can't believe someone was shooting at us in broad daylight," Marcus said. He glanced at the lane on his left. "We should call in the murder."

"And tell them what? That we just happened to be in the area when the guy died? It could get complicated really quickly, and we might end up holding the bag."

"And you are supposed to be the cop."

"I'm smart too."

"What about CCTV? It'll show we were there."

"No CCTVs in that area."

Marcus gave him a sharp glance. "How do you know?"

"That's cartel territory. And I checked."

Marcus whistled. "You don't say?"

"I didn't tell you 'cause I didn't want you to freak out."

"Like you just did."

"Oh, shut up. You were being slow and needed a 'little' motivation."

"Yeah, right."

They both stayed silent until they got closer to the city.

"Thank you," Marcus finally said.

"For what?" Dave asked.

"For back there."

There was no need to elaborate. Dave knew what Marcus was referring to. They'd been lucky. "Do you have someone to fix your windscreen?" he asked.

"I have a guy. He'll take care of it, thirty minutes tops."

"Okay, because we don't want Zora to find out what just happened."

"I agree. But what about the witness?"

"We have her picture. I have a friend who has a facial recognition software that can help us track her down."

"That works," Marcus said. "I'll take care of the windscreen and then stop by Zora's on my way home."

Zora hadn't told him, but Dave had guessed that Zora and Marcus had a history beyond what he knew. Yet it didn't matter. He trusted Zora. Marcus was her friend, and she needed all her friends around her now, but that didn't mean he liked it.

"Okay, just drop me off at the courthouse," Dave said. "I need to pick up my car."

Dave hadn't told Marcus, but he planned to circle back to the shady neighborhood later tonight after taking care of some stuff at his apartment. He was almost certain the witness would remain at the store until later tonight, when she could leave under the cloak of darkness.

Dave had no plans to let her disappear.

The man gazed at the young woman, who looked tiny and vulnerable as she lay sleeping on the hospital bed in the VIP wing of Lexinbridge Regional, the room's finishings indistinguishable from that of a five-star hotel, but he didn't care about all that. The girl was all that mattered.

An IV line ran down her left arm, and a respirator mask supplying pure oxygen covered her nose and mouth. The man watched with trepidation as her chest rose and fell in rhythm with the bedside monitors. He couldn't believe she was the same girl he'd taken to a city gala a month ago.

Mayor Williamson had received an urgent call from the hospital about his daughter, who'd presented three days ago at the ER complaining of abdominal pain. An examination and a few tests later, they'd admitted her, but her condition had worsened, so they'd transferred her to the ICU for close monitoring. Someone had realized who she was, and they'd called the mayor's office before transferring her to the VIP wing at his request.

Now the doctor was telling him that his daughter had both an aneurysm and an obstructing colorectal cancer, and she needed urgent surgery. His hands still shook from the news, but he masked it by gripping the bed rail.

"How soon can we have the surgery?" he asked the doctor standing beside him.

"The procedure required in this case is very complicated," Dr Thompson replied. The bespectacled surgeon had replaced Dr. Anderson as the surgery department chair. "Your daughter has two conditions that require separate major surgeries to address them. If we decide to repair the aneurysm before coming back to remove the tumor, we expose your daughter to the risk of tumor progression before we can take it out, since we'd be touching a major blood vessel in her body. If we remove the cancer first and schedule a second surgery for the aneurysm, the aneurysm might rupture before then, especially with one this size. The only other option is to take care of both of them in the same surgery."

"How soon can we schedule that?" Mayor Williamson asked. Doctors had reasons for explaining things in detail, but he wished the man could just go straight to the point.

"That's where we have a problem," Dr. Thompson said. "Only two doctors in this hospital have had significant experience with this kind of surgery. It's important to select the right doctor, given how risky the surgery is."

"Who are they? Let's get them in here," the mayor said.

Dr. Thompson exchanged a quick look with the attending that stood at his side before turning back to the mayor. "One of them is Dr. Edwards, whose death you must have seen in the news."

"Yes, I've heard about it," Mayor Williamson said. That was history. Why bother mentioning it? "So, he's out of the question. Who is the other doctor?"

"A fifth-year resident. But she has superior surgical skills, has worked extensively with Dr. Edwards on this topic, and has even handled a few cases on her own."

"Why are we wasting time? Let's bring her in."

Dr. Thompson cleared his throat.

"Go on. Tell me. Who is she?" The mayor wished this man would just hurry up and say the name.

"Dr. Zora Smyth."

"You mean—"

"Yes, the same Dr. Smyth accused of murdering Dr. Edwards."

Mayor Williamson sagged against the hospital bed in disbelief.

36

"There's another doctor with the relevant experience available in Boston," Dr. Thompson continued.

The mayor gave the man a hard look. He hated when professionals, including politicians, behaved like this. Why couldn't the doctor just say everything at once, instead of dishing it out piece by piece?

"He's on vacation in Alaska, but he doesn't have hospital privileges here or the license to practice in this state," Dr. Thompson said. "We can reach out and ask him to come, and then try to take care of the other issues. But it might take time, time your daughter may not have if the aneurysm ruptures, which is a possibility given how large it is."

The mayor stared far off for a few seconds. "Does

Dr. Smyth still have her license to practice?" he asked.

"Yes, she does," Dr. Thompson responded. "We've just revoked her hospital privileges, but it's easy to grant her a temporary one for this surgery, since she's already in the system." Dr. Thompson dropped his hands into the pockets of his medical coat. "I know you have a tough decision to make. Why don't I give you some time to think it over?"

The mayor nodded as he continued to observe his daughter.

Dr. Thompson glanced at the girl and then turned and left the private room with his attending.

The mayor kept his eyes on his daughter lying helplessly on the bed.

"What do you plan to do, sir?" his assistant by his side asked. "Asking Dr. Smyth to handle the surgery could mean political suicide, especially in the upcoming election. They've indicted her of murder."

"But she's not been convicted."

"The public doesn't care, sir," his assistant countered. "They'll bury you all the same. We'll be better off going with the doctor from Boston and fast tracking the approval process for him as much as we can."

The mayor stayed quiet, though he acknowledged

his assistant was right. He moved forward and perched on the edge of his daughter's bed and brushed tendrils of her dark hair away from her face.

Katherina. They'd grown close after her mother had died many years ago from a massive stroke. She was his only child, and he loved her so much. He hadn't done enough for her since her mother's death, yet she'd grown into a bright, intelligent young woman. He'd been so proud when she'd gotten her admission to law school a few weeks ago. Now here she was, fighting for her life. The mere thought of losing her was more than he could handle.

But his political career was also important—it was his lifelong dream. He'd invested many years of hard work to get to where he was today, and he still had some ways to go. Mayor Williamson was also planning to run for governor in the next term. Everything looked bright for him, yet a wrong move could tank his political career.

His next decision meant everything.

37

Zora sat on the couch in the living room and watched a surgical video on her laptop that the security team had retrieved from her apartment. Zora was grateful for the chance to continue brushing up her skills while she waited for the case to be resolved. The room had darkened somewhat from the setting sun, so she'd switched on the lamp on the side table.

For some reason, she'd been drawn to the OR video of the last colorectal case she'd handled with Dr. Edwards. The surgery had been especially difficult, but Dr. Edwards had complemented her on her skills. Zora had planned to apply for a colorectal fellowship at Lexinbridge Regional as soon as she completed her residency, so she'd been watching OR video recordings of complicated colorectal surgeries before they'd arrested her. Now that she was fired, Zora hadn't lost hope she'd return and finish what she'd started.

Christina lay on the sofa as she chatted with her mom on the phone. From what Zora overheard, her mom was having fun on her cruise and had even met a guy. Christina had vetoed the idea, teasing and warning her mom to be careful. Zora's mom had gone to the office to connect with the legal team she'd pulled for the case.

Zora's phone rang. She looked at the screen, and her heart dropped. It was a Lexinbridge Regional number. Were they calling her to give her the job back? If not, what else could it be?

"This is Dr. Zora Smyth," she said as she answered the call. She was still a doctor no matter what was happening; she'd earned it with her blood, sweat, and tears.

"Good evening, Dr. Smyth. This is Dr. Thompson from Lexinbridge Regional."

Zora's heart quickened. The department chair?

"Good evening," Zora responded.

"I'm sure you must be wondering why I called," Dr. Thompson said.

That was an understatement. She couldn't wait to hear what he had to say.

"Would it be possible for you to come to the hospital right away?" he asked.

Zora drew in a sharp inhale. "What is this about?"

"You'll find out when you get here, Dr. Smyth."

"I'm not sure that's a good idea right now, given what's happening."

"I can assure you no harm will come to you," Dr. Thompson said. "But it's important that you get here right away."

Could this be the answer to her prayer? Or was it something else? No answers came, but Zora knew one thing: she was going to go.

She let out a cleansing breath. "I'll be there in thirty minutes."

"Thank you, Dr. Smyth. Please come straight to my office as soon as you arrive. Goodbye." The call ended.

"Who was that?" Christina asked.

"The hospital. Give me one second. I need to call Silas."

Zora dialed Silas' number and put him on speaker. "Hello, Silas. The hospital just called and asked me to come in immediately. I think it's about a patient, given the urgency. I've already assured them I'd be there."

Silas sighed. "Zora, you need to be careful. They've already fired you. What else do they want?"

"I don't know. But I think I need to go."

"Okay, but you can't go alone. I want Christina and the security team to go with you."

"I don't need the security folks, Silas. It would draw more attention to me."

"Zora, that's non-negotiable, given how recognizable you are right now. Or would you prefer the security team babysat you at home?"

"I'll go with her," Marcus said. Zora looked up to see Marcus headed in her direction. She hadn't heard him enter the house.

"No, you can't come, Marcus," Zora said. "Your face is also all over the news from the pictures the reporters took at the hospital. You'll draw way more attention than I'd want. I'd like to keep it as low profile as possible."

"How about I have two of the security detail go with you besides Christina?" Silas said. "That's the best I can do. Does that work?"

"I can live with that," Zora said. "Okay, I have to go, since they're waiting for me."

"Be careful, Zora," Silas said.

"I will. Thanks." She disconnected the call.

Zora turned to Marcus and Christina. "I think I'm all set," she said. She placed her laptop in its backpack and slung the bag over her shoulder. "Christina, let's go."

"I'll walk you guys out," Marcus said.

38

"What have you done?" Stewart's father bellowed, fury written all over his face as he sat in his usual spot at the dining table, with Vaslav standing on his right. The old man picked the vase on the table and threw it at Stewart's head, but Stewart dodged, and it hit the wall-papered wall behind him.

A sense of uneasiness filled Stewart. This wasn't what he'd expected when he joined his father for dinner. It was rare to see his old man like this. Heads had rolled the last time his father had been this way. "What do you mean?" he asked.

"You killed one of Jimmy Francone's men."

What was his father talking about? He'd ordered nothing of the sort.

His father pointed at Stewart's face. "I thought you assured me you were going to handle this Zora business. So tell me, how were Jimmy's men able to trace your so-called witness to one of our important shops? Now all his attention is on our turf, because your guy killed one of his key men."

"But I did not…" Stewart noticed the smirk on Vaslav's face, and he understood what had happened.

Vaslav had set him up and engineered everything to make it look like Stewart had done it.

The muscle in Stewart's jaw twitched. The shooter was as good as dead. Stewart did not suffer disloyalty, and anyone who'd betrayed him in the past had met a watery grave. But right now, he needed to defuse his father's anger.

His father banged his fist on the table. "I know Jimmy is going to do everything to take over that spot in retaliation. We can't afford a war with him right now, not with everything going on. We don't need any extra attention from the cops or the Feds on us." His father glared at Stewart. "You're going to take your hands off this matter. Vaslav is going to handle it from now on."

Stewart gave his father a tight smile and said nothing. When had Stewart ever done everything his father asked? Zora belonged to him—there was no way he was going to let her out of his control. But he didn't have to alert anyone to his plans.

"Leave me," his father commanded, and turned his attention to the newspaper in front of him. The conversation was over.

Stewart whirled and stormed out of the room. Dinner had been ruined, all because of Vaslav. The man would pay for what he'd done. Stewart had handled him so far with kid gloves, but since he'd humiliated Stewart in front of his father, all bets were now off.

Stewart strode toward the house's front door. Erik fell into step beside him.

"I need you to find three disposable guys to burn Vaslav's three houses down," Stewart said in a tight tone. Eric nodded. "Then you find him." Stewart was referring to the betrayer in his group. Erik nodded again and sprinted out of the house.

Stewart stopped short to see his so-called sister in a black A-line dress headed toward him.

"Hello, Thomas," she said with a smile.

Stewart glared at her. He hated that saccharine smile—it made him want to puke. He had a strange urge to wipe it permanently off her face, but his father would go berserk if he did so now. How could she be so oblivious to the fact that he wanted to wring her neck anytime she called him by that name? He couldn't wait for the day he could get rid of her. Carving up her beautiful skin would be worth the years he'd endured her. Then his eyes shifted to the one-eyed chihuahua she held, and his anger melted a little. Sparky gave him a small bark.

Alisa didn't know how lucky she was that she had Sparky. He was the only thing about her he liked, and the other reason he hadn't harmed her over the years.

"Is everything okay?" Alisa asked.

Then Stewart remembered what had just happened, and his anger returned. "I'm fine," he said brusquely and brushed past her, leaving her standing there.

"Thomas—"

"What?" he growled.

Her eyes search his face. "Never mind. Maybe some other time."

Stewart turned and kept walking. If she knew what plans he had for her, she'd never interrupt him again and would stay far away instead.

He left the house, got into his car, and drove like a madman out of there. He needed to be alone, and only one place would do.

Soon, he arrived at a secret hideout no one knew about, not even Erik. He'd found an unoccupied house next to Zora's mother's. The couple was on some extended vacation around the world. From here, he had a clear line of sight to Zora's bedroom and the front of the house.

Stewart had spent last night here since they'd released her on bail, watching her sleep. Luckily, he was not on call this week, and so he'd planned to do the same today. But he was here early.

He picked up the binoculars from the small table that leaned against the wall, pulled up a chair, and sat down. He looked through the binoculars and scanned the view. There were no movements in her bedroom. That wasn't unusual, since it was still early yet. He turned his attention to the front door, and it opened at that moment.

Stewart leaned forward. There was the unmistakable figure of Zora coming out of the house, followed by Christina and Marcus. They stood there and talked for a few minutes, though Stewart was too far away to hear what they were saying. Then he saw Marcus give her a long hug before releasing her.

Stewart's nostrils flared, and a muscle in his jaw spasmed. What gave Marcus the right to hug her? Zora was his and his alone. He'd planned to get rid of

Dave and Marcus later, but he was tired of seeing this guy around Zora.

He didn't care what his father thought.

It was time to change things up.

oraentered the hospital with Christina and the security detail trailing behind her. She could feel eyes on her, but she ignored them and looked straight ahead. Most of the hospital staff were gone for the day, and visiting hours were over, which was perfect for Zora. She didn't need any unnecessary attention.

She headed toward the elevators and soon reached the fourth floor. The few medical staff who recognized her averted their eyes.

A stab of pain pierced Zora's heart. This was what she'd expected, but that didn't mean it hurt any less. She schooled her features and continued straight ahead. Dr. Thompson's office was on the far right of the east wing, the same office that his predecessor, Dr. Anderson, had occupied.

Zora stepped into the front office. The secretary, Julie, was absent from her seat, which was unusual. Julie liked to wait for her boss to close for the day before leaving. Zora figured Dr. Thompson had sent her home. She wondered who the patient was to demand such privacy.

Zora pulled her medical coat and stethoscope from her backpack, donned it, and handed her backpack over to Christina.

"I'll wait here with them," Christina said and gave Zora's hand a small squeeze before letting go.

Zora nodded and knocked on the door to the inner office. She heard a faint reply, and she entered the large office.

The office looked different, even though she'd only been here a few weeks ago. Books and journals arranged in neat lines lined the bookshelves with nothing out of place. The maple desk had small stacks of paper arranged on one side, with colorful pens resting in their own bin, instead of the disheveled mess Dr. Anderson's had been. The floor of the office was devoid of obstacles, and Zora now noticed the dark blue carpeting that covered the area.

Dr. Thompson sat behind his desk while another

man in a crisp suit stood looking out the only window in the room.

"Come in, Dr. Smyth," Dr. Thompson said and gestured to a visitors' chair. The man at the window turned at his voice, and Zora's eyes widened.

It was the mayor. Zora had only seen him on TV, and he looked younger, taller, and more dashing in person.

Zora sat down. What was he doing here? Was he the patient?

The mayor walked over to where Zora sat and took the other available chair. He turned and cast a set of startling gray eyes on her. "Dr. Smyth, let me get straight to the point," he said. "I need you to save my daughter."

Zora looked in confusion from the mayor to Dr. Thompson. "What's going on?" she asked. "I thought you'd fired me."

Dr. Thompson pulled at his shirt collar. "Yes, we did do that. But there's a patient that needs your urgent help, and you're the only one that can handle it."

Hope swelled in Zora's heart. Maybe this was the answer to her prayer. "Does this mean I'm rehired?"

"Well, this is just temporary," Dr. Thompson said,

dashing Zora's hopes. "But we've restored your hospital privileges."

Zora felt a little disappointed. But it was a positive step, nevertheless. Besides, she could never turn down a patient who needed her help.

She turned back to the mayor. "What's wrong with your daughter?"

"I think it's best if you see her for yourself," Dr. Thompson said.

———

Zora stood by the bedside and looked down at the frail girl. She'd expected a much younger child and was surprised the mayor had a daughter this age. The nurse confirmed the girl had woken up for a few minutes, but the pain meds had sent her back to sleep. Zora had read her case file and then examined her.

It was uncommon to see a girl this young with colorectal cancer and even rarer to see it complicated by a large aneurysm extending from the descending aorta into the iliac region. But Zora had seen worse and was confident she could handle the case. Yet the surgery had to be soon. The girl was like a time bomb waiting to explode.

Now she knew why she'd wanted to review the

OR video case earlier today. Who would have known that what she'd reviewed would be very relevant to this case? She sent up a silent prayer of thanks.

"What do you think?" the mayor asked her. Zora hadn't noticed when he reached her side. His demeanor had changed, a softer side to him exhibiting itself, the kind she expected of a parent worried about his precious child.

Zora turned to him. "We need to get her into the OR as soon as possible. But it's going to be a long and complicated surgery. There's a high risk of mortality in this kind of surgery, even with the best of experts. I'm more worried about that aneurysm rupturing either before or during the surgery, since it could mean instant death if it happens. Then there are other typical risks associated with surgery.

"For the surgery, we're going to cut off the section of the colon affected by the cancer to take out as much of the tumor as we can, and then we'll reconnect the healthy tissue. We'll do this while repairing the aneurysm at the same time.

"After the surgery, she'll undergo chemotherapy and a new proton beam radiation therapy that seems to work well for children and young adults in targeting cancer cells while sparing healthy tissue. There's additional information on all the risks detailed in the paperwork we'll give you to review and sign. But we'll do our best to take care of her." She turned to Dr. Thompson. "Let's schedule it for early tomorrow morning. The sooner, the better for her."

Dr. Thompson nodded to the attending beside him, who left to make the arrangements.

"Thank you," the mayor said. "I'll leave her in your hands."

Zora gave him a small, encouraging smile. Here he was, just like any other parent who had a sick child.

But taking on this case was also a huge responsibility. If the girl died on the table, the mayor would not hesitate to prosecute Zora for murder. Zora had no choice but to do her best, as always.

"I have to go to the office now," the mayor said to Dr. Thompson. "I'll be back in the early hours of the morning."

An erratic blare from the monitors pierced the air.

40

"What do you mean?" Zora's mom asked the court-qualified forensic scientist on the other end of the line. Adrianna was in a conference room with her legal team, and all fifteen pairs of eyes from around the large conference table stared at her. Silas sat in a black swivel chair beside her. Her team had been working non-stop for the past twenty-four hours, and she could tell most of them were tired. They needed a miracle soon.

"In layman's terms, the latent impression of the fingerprints on the scalpel differed from what we expected," the articulated voice said from the other end of the line. "For example, a fingerprint found on a bathroom sink has a different configuration from one found on a bedside table due to differences in surface texture. The ones we found on the scalpel were from a porcelain or ceramic surface."

"Like a mug?" her mom asked.

"Exactly."

Zora was a coffee connoisseur, and anyone who watched her enough would know she liked to visit the café near her apartment. Whoever had framed her could have lifted her prints from one of many mugs she'd used there. The mug could have also come from her apartment or from the hospital.

Adrianna's heart sped up. This might be the break they'd been searching for. Her team had found little to no new information in the large boxes the prosecutor had sent over. Adrianna had been ready to call him and give him a piece of her mind when the forensic lab called.

"Is this information strong enough to take before a judge?" she asked.

"Absolutely. I'm surprised the prosecutor missed this. Let me put together a detailed report about this and other findings and have it delivered to your office as soon as possible."

"I'll be waiting in the office for it. Thanks, Conrad."

"Always my pleasure, Mrs. Smyth. And you owe me two cups of coffee and a dinner now."

Adrianna chuckled. The man had been begging her since forever to go out on a date with him, but she always turned him down. Now it seemed he'd found a way in. "I'll make good on it once the case is all over," she promised.

"I'll hold you to it. Goodnight, Mrs. Smyth."

"Thanks again, Conrad." The line disconnected.

"What was that all about?" Silas asked.

"The lab found evidence that could save Zora."

The room erupted in clapping and high-fives. Silas squeezed her hand in encouragement.

Adrianna raised her hand, and the room went silent. "It's still not going to be enough. We need to find more corroborating evidence that we can take to the judge."

An attorney raised her hand.

"What is it, Rachel?" Adrianna asked. She was a quiet young lawyer they'd hired from a second-tier mid-western law school. The other partners had thought little of her, but Rachel had proved them wrong. Adrianna had been right to hire her.

"I looked into the make of the murder weapon. It turns out that this brand of scalpel is uncommon in this area."

Adrianna leaned forward. "Really?"

"Yes, it's not the make any of the hospitals or the medical stores carry."

"I want you to dig more into it. We might have something there."

"I'll take care of it and get back to you tonight."

"Okay. Good job, Rachel."

Rachel's face turned red to match her hair.

Adrianna smiled at her and then addressed the group. "Anything else?" she asked.

Peter, a blonde-haired lawyer that looked like he'd just graduated from college, spoke up. "My aunt got invited over to Mrs. Edwards' house, and I plan to go with her. Hopefully, we can get her to talk about what happened that day."

"Okay. Let me know how it goes."

"Yes, ma'am."

Adrianna's phone buzzed, and she glanced at the screen. It was an incoming call from Marcus. She turned to Silas. "Could you please handle the rest of the meeting? It's Marcus, and I need to take this call."

"Sure, I'll handle it."

Adrianna got up and strode out of the conference room. The door to an adjacent guest office was open, and she looked in to see the pale-blue-colored room was empty. She stepped in, shut the door behind her, and then leaned against the empty desk.

"Hello, Marcus."

"Hi, boss. I just got a call from a CI on my way back from your house. He's located the TPS courier guy."

Adrianna straightened. More good news. She loved how the day was shaping up. "Awesome. Where is he?"

"He's in a bed-and-breakfast outside the city. The CI said it seemed the guy was studying for some exam and had holed up there to prepare for it."

"When are you going to see him?"

"I'm on my way already. I'll let you know what I find out."

Adrianna's shoulders relaxed. "This is superb news, Marcus."

"I know. It'll be awesome if the guy could serve as Zora's alibi." Adrianna heard a car horn blare in the background. "Okay, I have to go. I had to park on the shoulder of the highway to make this call."

"What happened to your bluetooth headset?"

"I don't know. I can't find anything since Dave got in my car. He must have tossed it somewhere."

"Or more like Dave organized your mess."

"Hey, that hurts, Mrs. S."

Adrianna chuckled. Then she became serious again. "How was Zora at the house?"

"She just left for the hospital."

"Silas mentioned the hospital wants to see her."

"Yes, Zora thinks it might be about a patient."

"Thank goodness the security team went with her."

"Don't worry, ma'am. I'm sure she'll be safe."

Adrianna sighed. "I pray so." She smoothed her hair. "I feel like I've aged since I first heard about her arrest."

"It's going to be alright."

"I know. Make sure you take care of yourself, Marcus. We can't be too careful."

"I will. Talk to you later, ma'am."

"Bye." She ended the call and tucked the phone into her pants pocket.

The door to the office opened, and Silas stepped in and shut the door behind him.

"Any news?" he asked as he walked over to where she stood.

"Marcus found the TPS guy."

"That's great."

She smiled at him. "I know."

"How are you holding up?" he asked.

Adrianna closed her eyes for a moment and then opened them. Tears stung at the back of her eyes. "I can't lose her, Silas."

Silas pulled her into a hug.

She should have stepped away, since they were in the office, but Adrianna needed this hug. Besides, the room's blinds were pulled shut.

It was no secret Silas had been in love with her for many years, but Adrianna had erected a wall between them. Since she'd lost her daughter, and then her husband, she had this fear she'd lose him if she let him in. But Silas had stayed by her side, and with Zora's arrest, the wall had started crumbling.

"Everything's going to be okay," he said as he rubbed her back.

His touch was soothing, warming her insides and giving her the comfort she needed.

Silas held her away from him and stared into her eyes. "In fact, everything is already getting better."

She gave him a small smile. "I know, but I can't help how emotional I am right now."

He chuckled. "Don't worry about it. You're talking to good old Silas, your dearest friend." He leaned forward. "I won't tell your staff. We can't let anything happen to your 'iron lady' image," he whispered and winked at her.

Adrianna laughed. He knew just what to say to make her feel better. "Thanks, Silas."

"You're welcome," he said. "Now what was Conrad trying to finagle from you?"

Adrianna chuckled. "He wasn't that bad. Just that I owed him dinner and coffee."

"I think it's time I had a chat with that old coot."

"Oh, leave him alone. One dinner is nothing compared to getting my daughter back."

"Are you sure? I'm pretty certain he's going to tell the whole world about it."

"Would you like to come along?"

Silas lifted an eyebrow at her. "Free dinner from you? How can I turn it down?"

Adrianna laughed. "You're incorrigible."

"I can do better than that."

She stepped away from him. "It's time to get back to work. If we keep digging, we might just get enough to take to the judge."

"I've already requested to see him."

Silas, always thinking ahead. This was one thing she liked about him. "Thank you," she said.

"My pleasure."

Adrianna strode toward the door, with Silas following behind.

She prayed the miracle would continue, and they'd gather enough evidence by tomorrow.

Because she needed everything to be over, for Zora's sake.

41

M arcus trudged up the front steps that led to his apartment building. He was exhausted. All he wanted to do now was have a quick dinner, wait for news about Zora's safe return to her mother's house, and then go to bed. He'd have preferred to wait for her at her mom's place, but he needed to take a quick shower, and Dave had let him know he'd be there for her instead.

Marcus was disappointed when he'd found out Zora had a new boyfriend. Though he thought Dave was old school, Marcus could see he was one of the good guys. He didn't show it much, but it was obvious he adored Zora. Zora's mom had also confirmed they'd dated in the past, but Zora had been the one who broke the relationship when she'd withdrawn from everyone when her sister went missing. He was happy she was with someone who genuinely cared for her, though Marcus himself had missed out on Zora.

His whole body ached. He'd gotten a call from one of his informants about the location of the TPS courier man, while he'd been leaving Zora's mom's house. Marcus had met with him, and he'd corroborated Zora's story, which was fantastic news, and what the case sorely needed.

The case's progress had discouraged Marcus, but this ordeal had opened his eyes to how much Zora meant to him, and he needed was for her to be safe and sound. It didn't matter if she had another guy she loved; Marcus would cheer her on from the sidelines.

"Marcus Tate?" Marcus turned at his name to see a young man in a medical coat walking toward him. He didn't recognize the fellow. Was he one of Zora's colleagues?

He heard a loud crack and felt a sharp pain hit his chest as he fell back. Marcus landed on his knees and looked down to see blood seeping down his shirt. He glanced at the shooter, only to see him shed his medical coat as he walked away. So it'd been a ruse to make him let down his guard.

Marcus tried to stand, but he couldn't. He placed

his hand over the area to staunch the blood, but it was futile—the blood flowed even more. His breath came in quick gasps, and he found it hard to breathe. Marcus tried to reach for his briefcase—his phone was in it—but he couldn't get to it as his limbs grew weak, and the pain in his chest overwhelmed him.

He crumbled on the steps and watched his blood drained away, helpless to stop it.

Marcus knew without being told that he was dying. His only regret was the grief it would bring Zora, which was the last thing she needed. He wouldn't even be around to see the case dropped. *I'm sorry, Zora*, he said silently.

Then his world dimmed.

42

"BP is crashing!" a nurse called out.

Zora grabbed a pair of gloves and glanced at the monitor's screen. The patient's blood pressure was dropping, though her heart remained in sinus rhythm.

"What's going on?" the mayor cried out.

Zora motioned to one of two nurses who had rushed in with a crash cart, and she escorted the mayor out of the room, while Zora reached out and increased the flow of the IV line connected to the patient.

She donned the gloves and examined the patient's abdomen. It was guarded, and there were no bowel sounds on auscultation—not good. She grabbed a sterile syringe, plunged it into the abdomen, and drew red blood. Patient was bleeding into the abdomen. She hoped the aneurysm hadn't ruptured, though she would have expected the blood pressure to drop a lot in that case. But this patient still needed to get into the OR ASAP. "We need blood and frozen plasma stat," she said.

"They're on the way," a nurse confirmed.

"Let's elevate the foot of the bed." Another nurse responded to the instruction.

"V-fib!" the first nurse called out.

Zora took a quick look at the monitor. The rhythm was all over the place. "CPR," she called out. A nurse had already started pumping the patient's chest.

"I'll handle the code," a familiar voice said. Zora turned to see Brian by her side. She gave him a brief smile. "Paddles ready? One hundred joules," he shouted.

"Everyone, step back!" a nurse yelled as she placed the defibrillator paddles on the patient's chest.

The paddles discharged, and the patient reacted.

Zora glanced again at the monitor. The sinus rhythm was back, but systolic blood pressure was now at sixty.

"We have blood and frozen plasma," a nurse cried out.

"Let's put them up," Zora said. The nurse complied.

Zora watched as each drop of blood slid down the IV line to the patient's arm. "What the systolic now?" she asked.

"Ninety," a nurse called out.

"We can go with that for now. Good work, everyone." She turned to Brian. "Could you help me watch her? I'll be right back."

"Go, I'm here," Brian said.

Zora strode out of the VIP room. Dr. Thompson stood outside the door with the mayor.

"How's she doing?" the mayor asked, worry lines furrowed on his forehead.

"We've been able to stabilize her, but we need to get her into the OR now instead of tomorrow," Zora responded.

"Isn't that risky?" the mayor asked. "Can she handle surgery now, considering what just happened?"

"There's no guarantee she won't have a repeat episode if we wait until tomorrow. There's some internal bleeding going on, and we need to stop it as soon as possible," Zora said.

The mayor glanced at Dr. Thompson, who

nodded in agreement. The mayor sighed. "Give me whatever paperwork I need to sign."

Dr. Thompson signaled to a nurse, who led the mayor away.

Zora turned to Dr. Thompson. "I'll need a vascular surgeon to join me for the surgery and an attending from our service to sign off on it."

"I'll sign off on the surgery." Zora turned in the voice's direction that had spoken. It was the attending who'd corroborated her story about the missing patients.

She gave him a brief smile, and he smiled back.

"I'll join you in the OR as well," he said. "And Dr. Brennan is the anesthesiologist on-call."

Perfect. Just her favorite person.

She turned back to Dr. Thompson. "I'll also want Christina as the scrub nurse," Zora said, and pointed to where she stood with the security detail.

"Done," Dr. Thompson said.

Zora relaxed. She had a good team going in with her. "We're all set. Let's get her to the OR," she said and headed back into the patient's room.

It was time to get down to business.

Because this surgery tonight could make or break Zora's life.

The intermittent beep from the cardiac monitors reigned in the atmosphere.

They'd transported the patient to the OR and placed her under controlled hypotension. Zora stood on her right side, while the vascular surgeon and the attending stood on the left. Fortunately, she'd worked with the vascular surgeon before on a case like this, and the three of them had done a quick verbal run-through of the surgery before heading into the OR. Zora was sure there were other surgeons in the surgical conference room, watching on the video screen via the camera. It was time to begin the surgery.

She said a quick prayer and made the first cut. Zora stayed quiet and focused, working quickly and efficiently. The other surgeons remained in sync, and Christina did great in anticipating their needs.

A call came through into the OR, and the surgical tech picked the call. "Dr. Smyth, it's a call for you," she said.

"What is it?" Zora asked, without looking up.

"It's the ER. A Mr. Marcus Tate was brought in for gunshot wounds, and you're listed as his emergency contact."

Zora froze, and she took a sharp inhale. It couldn't be. She'd seen and spoken to Marcus about an hour ago. But the ER wouldn't be lying. It had to be Marcus. Someone had hurt him!

Zora fought back the tears and struggled to maintain her focus. There was no way she could leave her patient on the operating table, no matter how much she wanted to run to Marcus. *God, I need you to take care of him.*

"What should they do?" the surgical tech asked.

"Tell them to page Dr. Brian Atkinson. He'll handle it on my behalf."

She forced back her focus to the patient on the operating table. Zora could feel Christina's eyes on her, but this wasn't the time to be distracted. *God, help me keep it together. Please keep him alive.*

It was the best she could do.

Zora hoped it was enough.

43

D ave stepped out of his car and scanned the area around Zora's apartment. Nothing seemed out of place—it was business as usual. Mothers pushed their kids in strollers, and young business professionals returned home from work. A few teenagers loitered on the street, but they soon headed for the cafe around the corner.

He didn't even know why he'd bothered coming back here, but something had niggled at the back of his mind about this place, like there was a riddle here he needed to solve. Unfortunately, he didn't know what he was looking for. But experience had taught him not to ignore this feeling whenever it hit.

Dave walked down the street, but nothing caught his attention. Soon he arrived at an alley across the street, close to where Zora's building stood. He stepped into it and noticed there was a car parked there.

Wait! This car hadn't been here when he'd searched the area after Zora's arrest.

Dave circled the car. Thick layers of dust covered its surface, as if the car had been untouched for quite some time. But there were recent tire threads as well, running in and out of the alley, an alley that had been empty the last time Dave was here. The best part was the dash camera that stared Dave back in the face.

He stood at the alley's entrance and looked out into the street, where he could clearly see the front of Zora's building!

Dave's heart raced. Was it possible that the dash camera had captured the entries and exits for the day in question? Maybe the owner had moved the car after the incident—which could account for why he hadn't seen it on the day he came—but then returned it after a few days later.

There was only one way to find out.

Dave snapped pictures of the license plate and the car and sent it to a colleague of his at the station, who'd always helped him out. They'd been friends even before he joined the Lexinbridge police force, and he agreed to help Dave locate the owner. Dave hoped the effort would yield good news.

He left the alley and headed back to his car.

It was time to go back after the supposed witness.

———————

Dave hid in the shadows on the opposite side of the street in the run-down neighborhood and waited for the witness to come out. He'd changed and was now dressed in all black with a gun in his holster and a knife strapped to his ankle.

He looked at his watch. It was almost eight p.m., and he expected the witness to make her move soon.

True to form, the door of the store opened, and a figure stepped out, dressed in a black T-shirt over yoga pants, her black hair pulled into a ponytail. The woman hurried down the street, and Dave followed her, careful not to get too close and staying alert to his environment.

Soon she arrived at a much busier street and hailed a taxi. A yellow cab stopped at the curb, and she hopped in.

Dave flagged down the next cab he saw and slid in. "Follow that taxi," he said.

"You got it," the middle-aged driver replied and sped off in pursuit.

Dave followed the other cab until they arrived in a middle-class neighborhood. *Maybe she's going home*, Dave thought.

The first cab stopped in front of a small blue house with white shutters, and the woman got out. Dave asked his driver to drop him one street over, and he doubled back just in time to see a large man with a meaty head open the front door. He exchanged greetings with the woman, who then stepped into the house.

Dave's heart fell. Maybe she'd really returned home, but it didn't hurt to check.

He studied the house. It looked just like any other home on the street—quiet, with a manicured front lawn. He didn't see any security cameras, but that didn't mean there wasn't one. But he needed to confirm what was going on in the house.

He waited for any further movements, and crossed the street when there was none, staying in the shadows until he was at the side of the house. He looked at all the windows, but they appeared locked with the shades drawn.

Dave sighed. Maybe this was just a wasted trip.

Then he heard laughter coming from the back of

the house. Dave rounded the corner and crept closer, his footfalls silent. He noticed a window at the back of the house was open, and cigarette butts littered its window ledge. Someone had wanted a smoke break.

Dave edged the window open a little more until he could pass his hand through, and then he shifted the curtain a little.

His body stiffened, and a muscle in his jaw twitched. He couldn't believe what he was seeing. Young girls who looked to be about fourteen years old were sprawled on the floor in various areas of the kitchen. Most had their eyes closed, but the few with open eyes looked stoned.

Dave saw the woman he'd been tailing use a syringe to draw some medicine out of what looked like a medical drug bottle. She walked over to a girl, tied a tubing on the girl's arm, and injected the drug into her arm. Then the woman straightened, kicked the girl, and laughed.

Bile rose in his throat at the scene before him. Whatever they were doing inside here was illegal.

But he'd found the loophole he needed.

Dave slipped away from the house and called it in.

44

Zora stripped off her surgical garb and scrubbed her hands before exiting the OR. Christina wasn't out yet, though Zora's security detail stood waiting.

The surgery had been a success. All they had to do now was watch the girl for the next forty-eight hours. She'd supervised the patient's transfer to the recovery room, and now all of her attention had turned to the ER.

Marcus. She'd received no updates since they'd first informed her about him, and she hoped he was okay. She hurried down the hallway and took the elevators to the first floor. The sound of feet behind her told her the security detail was not far behind.

Zora soon reached the ER and strode past its

central nursing station. Her eyes swept the area, and she saw someone who looked like her mom standing in front of a cubicle. Zora headed in that direction.

With her heart in her mouth, she soon reached the cubicle, and her mom turned. Zora noticed she had tears in her eyes.

Her heart skipped a beat. No, it couldn't be. Marcus was definitely alive. He had to be.

"Zora—"

"Where's Marcus, Mom?" Zora asked. "I need to see him."

"I'm sorry—"

Zora brushed past her mom and rushed into the cubicle. She noticed a sheet covered the body on the bed. *No! Please God, no.* She reached for the sheet and pulled it back, only to see Marcus lying still with his eyes closed.

Zora staggered, and her mom caught her. "The doctors tried their best, and Brian helped as much as he could, but Marcus had lost too much blood," her mom said in a tremulous voice.

"What happened?" Zora asked in a whisper.

"He'd just returned from seeing a potential witness when a man shot him in front of his apartment."

Zora leaned forward and touched his face. It felt

cold. *Sweet Marcus*. He looked beautiful even in death. She would never hear his laughter or his teasing again, and it was all her fault.

Zora felt a sharp pain in her chest, and she collapsed on the floor.

—————

Zora stood by the patient's bedside in the ICU and watched her sleep. The patient had woken up in the recovery room and was now in the ICU for observation for the next forty-eight hours. A lot could still happen, but Zora believed the patient would pull through.

Yet the news about Marcus' death whirled at the back of her mind. She still couldn't believe he was dead. Zora wished she was dreaming and hoped someone would wake her soon. She'd stayed with him for a while before allowing them to take his body away to the morgue for autopsy, and she'd followed it there. Christina had joined her, and they'd both mourned his loss. Dave had arrived at the morgue and then left to scout the area around Marcus' apartment for witnesses or any evidence that might help the case. Zora had eventually returned to the ICU.

A nurse came in to check the patient's vitals. "I'm so sorry for your loss," she said to Zora.

Zora acknowledged her with a nod. All the nurses and doctors she'd met since she returned to the ICU had said the same thing. Apparently, the news was all over the hospital grapevine, since she'd achieved celebrity status with her indictment.

The mayor had kept the press away from the hospital, and Zora was grateful for it. She didn't feel like talking to anyone, and the last thing she needed was cameras flashing in her face. All she wanted to do was mourn his loss in private.

The nurse finished attending to the patient and left. Zora yawned. She'd been sitting for a long time and needed to stretch her limbs. She got up and headed to the ICU waiting room where a water dispenser stood. Her security detail was there as well, and she flashed a brief smile at them. Zora grabbed a cup of water and strode back to the patient's cubicle.

She entered the room and saw a man in scrubs about to inject something into the patient's IV line. "Who are you?" Zora asked. "What are you doing?"

The man dropped the needle on the floor and raced toward Zora. Zora couldn't identify who he was, since he wore a mask. The man pushed Zora out of the way, and she fell against a cart in the corner. She inhaled sharply at the sudden flank pain.

"Security!" Zora screamed. "Stop that man." A flurry of running feet raced after him.

Zora rushed over to the patient's bedside. She let out a sigh of relief when she noted the steady rise and fall of her chest and the sinus rhythm that raced across the cardiac monitor's screen.

A nurse on duty ran into the room. "Are you okay?" she asked.

"We're fine," Zora said. "Did they catch the guy?"

The nurse shook her head as she checked the patient's vitals. "He ran away too fast, but the hospital's security team is combing the building for him. I've paged Dr. Thompson to let him know what just happened."

"Okay. Thanks."

"Let me know if you need anything." The nurse exited the room.

Zora sat on the single chair in the cubicle. Whoever that man was, he'd meant to harm the patient. Why?

Was it a vendetta against the mayor or against Zora? She couldn't tell. All Zora knew was she'd bear the consequences if anything happened to the patient.

She lifted her chin. Well, not on her watch. She was going to stay close until the patient was out of danger and transferred back to the VIP room.

Zora would not allow whoever was behind this to win.

45

U ncle Jimmy, a large man with equally large hands, shot up from his seat in his study. "What did you just say?"

"Someone murdered Marcus," the man who delivered the news said.

Uncle Jimmy picked the glass on his desk and threw it against the wall, where it smashed and then shattered into a million pieces on the floor.

The bearer of the bad news cowered.

"Get out!" Uncle Jimmy bellowed.

The man scurried out as fast as he could.

Uncle Jimmy banged his knuckles on the desk over and over again until they bled, but he didn't feel the pain.

His only family was dead. Gone.

Uncle Jimmy's vision narrowed, and the muscles and the veins of his neck strained against his skin.

He'd find Marcus' killer no matter what it took.

And make that person pay with his life.

46

"Charles, what's going on?" a familiar voice barked from the other end of the line.

Charles rubbed his eyes and looked at the time on his night-stand clock. No, he hadn't been dreaming. It was three a.m., and it was the DA calling him.

Charles sat up in his bed. "Good morning, sir," he responded. The DA was someone he couldn't mess with—his connections with Washington were rock solid.

"What's this about the Zora Smyth case? The mayor just called me, giving me an earful about it. You assured me the case was a slam dunk, and you had all the evidence. Now, why would I have to go through that because of you?"

Charles' heart sank. He was in deep trouble. The DA bore grudges against anyone who wronged him. "I'm sorry, sir," he said. "I'll take care of it."

"See that you do." The DA let out a sigh. "All eyes are on this case, Charles. If you are going full steam ahead, make sure you have all your ducks in a row. If not, close the case. We can't afford to be on the wrong side of this. This is your last chance. Don't mess it up."

"I won't, sir." The line went dead.

Charles dropped his phone on the nightstand and leaned back against the headboard.

This was killing him. If he dropped the case, the sponsor would not let him be. He didn't know what the man would do to vent his anger, especially since Charles had no idea who he really was—he'd never introduced himself, and his voice always sounded distorted on the phone.

But if Charles barreled ahead, and the case fell apart, the DA would bury him, which meant he could kiss his career goodbye.

He ran his hands over his bald head. This was a tough decision, and he only had a few hours to make up his mind.

47

Zora checked the patient one more time and then collapsed on the chair. She was exhausted. She'd stayed awake for most of the night, watching over her. The patient had remained stable and had woken up a few times.

The mayor had already come by to express his thanks to Zora for saving his daughter's life, and his security detail now guarded her cubicle, though they had to suit up in the ICU attire. Only Zora, the attending, the vascular surgeon, and two nurses assigned to the patient could see her, and Zora's close monitoring was no longer needed.

Zora left the ICU and headed toward the elevators. She needed a shower and fresh clothes. The elevator doors opened, and she saw Christina and Brian standing in it.

Her eyes widened. "What are you guys doing here?" she asked.

"We're here to get you before you collapse," Christina said. "Now, hop in."

Zora stepped in and pressed the ground level button. "But I'm fine," she said.

"No, you're not," Brian and Christina said in unison.

The corners of Zora's lips turned up. What was up with these two?

"Where are you going?" Christina asked.

"I need to grab some coffee and go see Marcus. I can't let him be all alone," Zora said.

"Zora," Christina said in a soft voice, "I was outside the autopsy room all night. They are working on him right now. He's not alone."

"Let's go eat instead," Brian said.

"I'm not hungry," Zora replied.

"But Marcus would want you to eat if he was here," Christina countered.

True. But he wouldn't want to be alone either, Zora mused.

The elevator doors opened on the ground floor. Christina grabbed Zora's arm. "You have no choice.

Come on." She pulled Zora out of the elevator and prodded her toward the ER.

"Isn't the cafe the other way?" Zora asked.

"You need somewhere quiet, and my car is in the ER parking lot," Brian said.

They arrived at a quiet cafe a few minutes away and were soon seated at a table. Zora noticed the only other occupants of the cafe were part of her security detail. So this was what they had been up to! She'd wondered where they'd gone when she hadn't seen them outside the ICU.

Their presence meant this was an arranged destination, but Zora didn't care. She stared out the window as Christina and Brian quibbled over what to order. Their bickering reminded Zora of Marcus, and tears burned at the back of her eyelids.

The food soon arrived, and Christina *oohed* and *aahed* over how delicious it was. But the food tasted like ash in Zora's mouth, and she only pecked at it.

It was still surreal that Marcus was dead. He'd often send her random notes of encouragement, which always seemed to arrive whenever she really needed them. Now she'd never see him again.

Zora felt a stab of pain in her heart. It was like her sister all over again. But while there was still hope she'd find her sister, Marcus was gone forever.

She choked back a cry. Zora felt a hand rub her back and looked up to see Christina's tear-filled eyes. Brian pretended to be interested in the food on his plate.

The pain of Marcus' death would eventually ease away, but for now, it was just hard to take.

Her phone buzzed in her medical coat pocket, and she pulled it out to answer it. "Hello, Mom."

"Zora, where are you?"

"I'm having breakfast with Christina and Brian."

"How are you holding up?" her mom asked softly.

"I'm okay."

"I still can't believe he's gone."

Zora said nothing. She was afraid the floodgates would open if she talked about Marcus.

"I have good news for you," her mom said.

"What is it?"

Zora listened as her mom spoke from the other end of the line and gasped.

48

"Zora, are you still there?" her mom asked.

"Yes, I am," she replied. She still couldn't believe her ears.

"The prosecutor has closed the case against you," her mom repeated.

The case was over. She had her life back, just like that.

"The DA's office had to drop the charges," her mom continued. "We got an independent forensic report to show that the fingerprints were planted—something about a latent impression being different depending on the texture of the surface it was lifted from. The scalpel was also a brand that was not typically used by any of the hospitals or carried in the medical equipment stores in this area. It also didn't

match any scalpel in your home or Dr. Edwards'
house.

"Dave found a car that had been parked for a
month in an alley close to your building's entrance.
Luckily, it had a dash cam, and it didn't show you
entering or leaving your apartment that day, except
when the cops took you away. A video from the
camera over the building's fire exit—the only other
door to the outside—which Dave's friend restored,
didn't capture you leaving as well.

Gratitude filled Zora's heart at all the work others
had done to make sure they'd set her free.

"Yet those alone wouldn't have been enough," her
mom continued. "The prosecutor's other witness
disappeared in the wind, and Dave caught their chief
witness committing another major crime, so her testimony was tossed out.

"But the clincher was the video file Marcus sent
to us before he was shot: a recording of the TPS
courier guy's testimony. I found the email this
morning and followed up with the guy, and he agreed
to testify in person if needed. He remembered how
nice you'd been to him that day. Dr. Edward's time of
death and the time he delivered the package matched,
so it ended up serving as your alibi. The mayor put a
lot of pressure on the DA's office to drop the case,

and since the evidence for your crime had become so weak, they had no choice but to close the case."

Marcus had come through for her from the grave. Her big brother had saved her.

Zora broke down and wept.

49

Stewart headed to his car in the hospital parking lot. He'd been on call and was bone-tired. The patients had run him ragged, and he couldn't wait to get the stink from the wards off his skin.

But he was furious at the turn of events. Of course, he was pleased that Marcus was no more, but the guys he'd sent to kill the girl that had tried to take Zora's life had failed. Idiots. When would they ever learn to do the job right? And now the prosecutor had called and informed him they couldn't hold Zora any longer, so they'd closed the case.

That creep. He'd disappointed Stewart again, despite all the money he'd pumped into the man's pocket. This was one reason why those with political aspirations couldn't be trusted. If Stewart could have managed it, he'd have donated the man's organs for the greater good. But he still had some use for him in the future, so he'd keep the prosecutor around until his value expired.

Stewart unlocked his car and got in. He needed to figure out a way to regain his grip on Zora, but his brain couldn't think of anything right now, short of kidnapping and whisking her away. That wasn't a bad idea, but it'd be hard to get to her right now, given her new security detail. They stuck to her like gum wherever she went.

He removed his medical coat, placed it on the front passenger seat, and started his car.

Suddenly, he couldn't breathe. Someone in the backseat held a garrote taut against his throat and was strangling him from behind. Stewart's hands clawed at the wire to remove it, but it held fast.

Whoever it was seemed intent on killing him.

Stewart reached out desperately to press the car horn, but the person behind him pulled the wire so tight it cut through his skin and made it difficult for Stewart to get the oxygen his brain needed.

His limbs flailed in their last struggle for survival.

"For Marcus," the man behind him whispered.

Then Stewart's lights went out.

EPILOGUE

Zora placed the flowers she'd brought on the grave. It'd been a week since Marcus' death, and they'd buried him a few days ago in the Smyth family's private lot, where Zora's father was laid to rest. She'd come with her mom to pay her last respects. The loss had hit her mom much harder than Zora had expected—it seemed Marcus had been like the son she'd never had.

The cops had caught his killer, who had ended up dead in a crossfire with the police. They'd identified him as a member of the same East European cartel that was behind the organ trafficking business. Dave had told her the word on the street was the cartel had taken a big hit from a rival group, so they'd gone into hiding. Zora was just glad they were no longer interested in her life.

The mayor's rating had soared since news of the case's dismissal broke—someone had leaked the details to the press. Dave's partner got demoted with a pay cut, and his boss was currently being investigated. Silas had reported there were rumors that Dave might step into his shoes. It seemed justice had prevailed, after all.

Her mom moved away to give her some privacy. Zora knew Marcus was in a better place, but that didn't mean she missed him any less. She brushed away the leaves that had fallen on the grave and sat down on the manicured grass beside the headstone. Zora missed his presence in her life and just wanted to spend the next few moments by his side.

She told him how the case against her had become old news—the press had lost interest in Zora once they'd cleared her the charges. Zora had gotten her job back to complete her residency. Her mom had threatened to sue the hospital for damages, but they'd settled and the hospital had signed an addendum to her employment contract. But Zora was just grateful to have her life back and the chance to become the surgeon she wanted to be.

Zora pulled out a letter her mom had given her on

their way to the cemetery. It had arrived at the law firm for her, and Zora now examined the envelope—there was no return address. But her mom had assured her that the security team had looked it over and declared it clean.

She opened the envelope and pulled out a single sheet that was nestled in it. Zora scanned the bottom of the letter—a Miss Kelly had signed it.

Her heart quickened. So Kelly was still alive. *Thank you, God.* She'd wondered what had happened to her after the attack in the communal shower. But why was she writing to her?

Zora started reading from the top.

Zora,

If you're reading this note, that means I'm out-of-the-country with my family, and my lawyers were successful in appealing my case as self-defense against an abusive husband.

You may be wondering why I'm writing to you. I wanted to tell you a little story, one you probably don't know about.

I first met your mother, Mrs. Smyth, in the courthouse after I was arrested for the murder of my husband. She'd come in for another case, but

she ended up staying in the wings for my arraignment. I was still in shock over what had happened and had blanked out during the session. I, a florist and home maker, had killed my husband after years of unimaginable abuse and only had a public defender on my side.

But your mother approached my lawyer and handed him her card. She said it was about the children. That was the wake-up call I needed. I snapped out of the shock and asked my lawyer to contact her. My husband's family was fighting for custody of my children, but I couldn't imagine those who had raised a monster like my husband rearing my kids.

Mrs. Smyth fought tooth and nail to make sure my mother gained custody. She helped my mother find a bigger apartment and paid off the rent for the next two years. She made sure my kids never missed a doctor's appointment, and when one of them ended up in the hospital at the time, your mother did everything to make sure she got better.

But I only found out later that your sister went missing during the time your mom helped us. I was racked with so much guilt and vowed to pay back the debt whenever the chance came. So imagine my surprise when I found out you were her daughter! I was out on a work detail when I saw Mrs. Smyth coming to pay you a visit.

That's why I tried to protect you as much as I could.

But that's not the main reason for this note. During my time in prison, I heard an inmate bragging about a child kidnapping that had made the headlines. It turned out the supposed kidnapping coincided with the time your sister went missing. I questioned the inmate, and she stated she had no idea where the girl had ended up, except she'd heard the girl was adopted by a rich family. The inmate was later murdered in prison.

I hope this information helps a little as you continue to search for your sister.

My regards to Mrs. Smyth. Please thank her again for shining a light of hope in my life.

My children and I send our regards.

Kelly

Zora's heart skipped a beat. Her sister. They'd been searching for her for so long, but all they'd had over the years were false leads that led nowhere. If this was true, maybe it could account for why they'd never been able to get any good leads on her whereabouts. It was like she'd dropped off the surface of the earth. And now Zora understood why her mom hadn't wanted to talk about Kelly—the memories reminded her too much of her sister.

She had to show her mom the note. Zora looked up and saw her mom standing a few feet away, staring off into the distance. Her face was ashen, like she'd seen a ghost, and her body shook.

Zora bid Marcus goodbye, got up, and hurried over to where her mom stood.

"Mom, what's wrong?" she asked. Her mom had always remained calm in most situations, so it was rare to see her so out of it.

Her mom continued shaking like a leaf.

Zora shook her mom's arm. "Mom, you're scaring me. What's going on?"

Her mom shook her head and grabbed onto Zora for strength.

"What is it? Tell me," Zora insisted.

"I think…" her mom said.

"Go on."

"I think I just saw your sister."

Thank you so much for reading!

Want to know what happens next to Dr. Zora Smyth? You can grab LETHAL RECONCILIATION at https://dobicross.com

If you've loved reading LETHAL OBSESSION, Dobi would be grateful if you could spend a few minutes to leave a review (as short as you like) on the book's page on your favorite retailer. Your review would help bring it to the attention of other readers. Thank you very much.

Check out all Dobi Cross books at https:// dobicross.com

ACKNOWLEDGMENTS

Writing a book is harder and more rewarding than I could have ever imagined. And it would not have been possible without the support, love, and encouragement from my number one cheerleader, my dearest mom. My life would never have been this awesome and wonderful without you.

Of course, I have to thank my precious little DC for his smiles and antics. You brighten my day and give me the strength to keep pushing through.

Thank you to my sisters for encouraging me on this wonderful journey. And a special thanks to my baby brother (who is so not a baby anymore) for being super supportive and checking in on my progress. You guys are the best.

Thank you to my wonderful author friends. You know who you are. Your selflessness and willingness to share what you know has made my writing journey smoother and an exciting one. And a special thanks to Lisa and Deanna whose support have made a difference.

Most of all, I want to thank God who gave me life, surrounded me with the most wonderful people, and loved me all the way. You make my life complete.

And finally, a special thanks to all my readers whose love of my stories spur me on to write more. Thank you!

ABOUT THE AUTHOR

As a former physician and business executive in another life—with a childhood filled with reading multi-genre novels (including Shakespeare in the original version)—Dobi Cross loves to write thrilling stories with heart.

She enjoys dreaming up everyday characters who rise above unfavorable circumstances to overcome incredible odds. When not writing, Dobi can be found binging K-dramas and ice cream with her little sidekick by her side.

Lethal Obsession is the third book in the Dr. Zora Smyth Medical Thriller Series. Sign up at https://dobicross.com to be notified when the next Dobi Cross book comes out!

Thanks for reading LETHAL OBSESSION!

https://dobicross.com
hello@dobicross.com
facebook.com/dobicrossauthor
bookbub.com/profile/dobi-cross
instagram.com/dobicross